VIKING'S DESIRE

Chapter 1

802

The longships snaked through the water as lithe as serpents, but the sea was rough. The men were wondering if the sea god Aegir would bless this voyage or curse it. Whenever the sun came out, a joyous cheer would erupt.

Both ships, Drakkars, were at least seventy five feet long with a fearsome looking dragon head at the bow, guiding their journey. Both Drakkars had sixteen pairs of oars with weapons stored near the crew's rowing positions. The crewman's sea chest doubled as their rowing bench and wrangling the huge ship was a demanding job. The men's lean muscles tensed with each passage of the great oars as they dipped into the sea and reached high into the sky before the process began again. They didn't seem to mind this grueling toil, even rejoiced in the pleasure of the sun, the ships, and the sea. It was, after all, a Norse tradition and each and every man was proud of their prowess and deep connection with Aegir.

The Viking shields decorating the side of the ship gave it even a more fearsome appearance. At times the wind would gust and they would be able to pull the oars into the ship through the slits by the oar holes and let the wind push the ship to the journey's end. The trip had been five days of rough seas and miserable rain, a truly arduous voyage, but nothing these battle-hardened, seasoned sailors were not used to. One day the crew heard the words they were waiting for, "Let the ravens fly," but the birds never returned to the ship, the significance of that being land. The expected first cry of "sea gulls" brought about a raucous cheer and everyone knew that the time was afoot. They were near land and their reason for coming here was at hand, Saxon riches. This was not the first time they had set foot on English soil. Most of Eriik Thorennson, Jarl of Jaedon's encounters with the Saxons had left him unimpressed. Eriik considered one battle and only one battle with the English interesting. The participants of that battle had been English knights. He considered only these knights worthy combatants, but the country in general was fair game to enrich the Norse coffers. Their land was rocky and cold most of the year. They needed these raids to supplement the treasury. Besides, they were Vikings and it was in their nature to go raiding. It had been passed down since Eriik was a small boy and even before. They had always raided to the east in the past, but in the last several years, since Eriik had been in charge, they had found the way to travel west, to the Saxon lands. Eriik was always thirsty for knowledge of this land. Familiarity was key in order for their raids to be successful. It was an advantage he had acquired from a slave he claimed from one of the first raids carried out on a monastery in England from an island called Lindisfarne. The priest he had taken home from that raid had not only taught him the English language but gave him understanding of the Saxon land he needed. Everyone in the Norse village thought him a complete dolt for picking a priest over silver and gold, but it turned out to be an ingenious choice. The priest knew not only of English lands and riches, but facts and wisdom that turned out to be precious to the Viking raiders. By the time two raids had been completed, Eriik's expertise had yielded the Norsemen five times more gold and silver than any of the previous raids together. He was famous and heralded among them as being exceptionally wise, and so he was, through knowledge. They were a superstitious race and felt as if a sea journey would surely fail without Eriik, that the gods were benevolent toward him. This was the third journey but the most perilous by far. They were sailing with two longships, doubling the risk. A monastery was not the easy target this time. Their destination was a castle further inland. This held danger twofold, they would have to cross over land, and castles were usually defended by the knights Eriik respected. But the Norsemen had the god Thor on their side. He had brought them here safely and that was a good sign. They had no doubt they were the

better warriors than even the English
knights. They were ready, and the riches
were there for the taking.

The longships anchored just outside the
reefs and the landing boats were launched.
Although the longships could actually beach,
it was not safe to do so. Sentries were
left on board to protect the precious ships.
The landing party gathered on the beach with
their weapons and shields, and if they had
been spotted, it would have brought terror
to the bravest of souls. They indeed looked
like demons from hell. These men were tall
and muscular and aching for a fight. Some
had swords and bows and arrows. Others had
swords and axes, but all were heavily armed
and knew exactly how to wield their weapon.
No Norseman was afraid to die, instead
welcoming it as each warrior would travel
swift and straight as an arrow to be
welcomed into the Halls of Valhalla with
open arms if they found death in battle.
Freya, the Goddess of Love and Beauty would
show them the way.

They were looking for a suitable camp site
between the beach and the castle, so at the
cock's crow they could walk the distance
while Sol, the god who drives the sun
chariot, would make only one rotation across
the sky, before they reached their
destination.

Chapter 2

English Countryside

The morning began at Castle Devorn as usual and proceeded as every other day except for the fact that Lillian could feel a tension she couldn't explain. It must be that horrid Lord Montfort. *Oh God, the way he leered at her made her blood run cold.* Whenever he touched her with his cold, damp hand, she winced and sometimes felt as if she would actually vomit. *Why won't he leave?* He'd been there far too long. She knew of her mother's hopes and political dreams and understood she anticipated help from Lord Montfort. Why her mother thought the lord would support her aspirations Lillian had no idea, but how she wished he would keep his mind on the business at hand and leave her alone!

In the drawing room, Lord Frederick and Lady Beatrice were in a heated argument about their only daughter. She was of marrying age and that was the subject at hand. Lillian was lovely with long, thick, sable hair with fiery auburn highlights and the deepest emerald eyes. Frederick loved her with all his heart. She was his little girl and she had him wound around her little finger since the day she was born. Her mother, on the other hand considered Lillian a way to bring status and esteem onto the house of Devorn.

Their guest, the wealthy Lord Simon Montfort had made his intentions very clear when he offered his hand in marriage for Lady Lillian to her father. Lord Devorn was a minor Lord, whereas Lord Montfort was powerful, with wealth and prestige. He knew the King of Wessex himself, King Egbert, and even had his ear, or so it was said. An alliance with Lord Montfort would be a coup in itself, and could open up worlds Beatrice had only dreamt of; power for her husband and herself, riches, even invitations to the royal palace perhaps. Visions such as these made her giddy with greed. After all, she deserved that kind of life, not this tedious country life filled with pigs, goats and lowly peasants. Lady Beatrice didn't see how they could turn down such a grand proposition.

"But my dear, I promised Lillian I would only give her hand in marriage out of love. She doesn't love Montfort, in fact, she can barely tolerate being in the same room with him."

"Love." Beatrice practically spat the word. "When does love make a good match? Why she's too young and silly to even know what she wants, certainly not to make a momentous decision such as this. Lord Montfort is wise, wealthy, influential, and can give our Lillian anything and everything she could ever want."

"Except love." Frederick was saddened by the thought.

Beatrice decided to try a different tact, "Darling, I know we both want Lillian to be happy. I personally think that after she gets used to the idea, she will be, but let's look at this from a different perspective, shall we? We really have no choice. She is of marrying age. No other suitor equal to Lord Montfort has asked for her hand in marriage. She turns her snooty little nose up at all of them anyway. Instead she keeps herself buried in her books in the library or staring starry-eyed from the tower. This kind of match doesn't come along every day and just think what political influence we could acquire. Isn't it our duty to do the best for our only daughter? Perhaps she will be happy with the proposal when she really thinks about it. Besides, do you want us to be stuck out here in the middle of the country our entire lives, missing out on all the grand balls and…oh my." Her eyes filled with tears, *crocodile tears.*

"Beatrice, I'm so sorry. Please don't cry. Perhaps a conversation with Lillian wouldn't hurt."

She ran her fingernails provocatively up and down Frederick's arm and he melted in her embrace, as expected.

"Frederick, darling, I knew you would see the sense in it after all."

★★★★

During the meal, Lord Montfort insisted on sitting right beside Lillian, ruining her appetite, as usual. Well, she would try to get a few bites down and then retire to her suite. Maybe if she just looked the other way, perhaps focusing on the hounds begging for scraps, anything! After eating just about everything she could without gagging, she turned to her mother and attempted to excuse herself but her mother wouldn't hear of it. As much as sitting next to that vile man was becoming quite a task, she couldn't disobey. The meal seemed to go on for an eternity when finally Lord Montfort excused himself and to her delight, retired to his suite quite unexpectedly.

Beatrice patted her hand and whispered, "Lillian darling, your father and I need a word privately. Would you join us in the drawing room?"

"Of course, Mother." She couldn't help but roll her eyes, behind her mother's back of course.

They entered the drawing room, the door closed, and her mother turned to Lillian with a gleam in her eye, "As your mother, you know that I only have your well-being at heart, as does your father."

Lillian would have loved to ask her mother when her well-being had ever been in her mother's heart, and exactly what heart was she speaking of anyway, but decided better of it. Instead she asked, "What's on your mind mother? I have things I need to do."

Beatrice said strongly, "Don't interrupt me when I'm talking to you young lady.

"As I was saying, we have your best interest at heart and that's why Lord Montfort is staying with us, at least part of the reason. I'm sure you've been wondering why an important man such as he would be so kind as to spend this much time with us and it's high time you knew.

"What does Lord Montfort staying with us have anything to do with me?"

Frederick cut in, "Listen to your mother sweet pea."

Beatrice continued, "Lord Montfort, as you know, is a powerful and wealthy, as well as inspiring man. This will be a wonderful opportunity for you as well as myself and your father."

"Mother, you can't possibly be talking about that repulsive creature with the damp, cold hands. He looks like a weasel! And *again*, what could he possibly have to do with me anyway?"

"Lillian, I'll have no disrespectful talk about a brilliant man such as the lord. Now mind your manners and let me continue and you'll understand if you could hold your tongue for a few precious moments." She straightened the bodice on her gown and cleared her throat, putting the smile back on her skillfully made up face. "You see my darling, he has made a very generous offer to help your father build some very influential contacts, along with other, shall we say, arrangements, which will develop into some grand appointments for your father and myself.

"Why exactly would Lord Montfort do such a thing to help us? We hardly know him."

"Well, that's what I'm trying to explain to
you. It would be because of our familial
kinship, dear."

"Familial? What on earth are you talking
about mother!"

Lillian started feeling ill. She couldn't
believe where her mind was going, such a
thing couldn't even be a possibility, she
wouldn't let herself turn down that path.
It had to be something different than what
was sweeping through her mind.

Her mother continued, "We will be related
soon. That's what I meant by an amazing
opportunity for you my darling. You see,
the lord, such a fine man, has asked your
father for your hand in marriage. I can't
imagine a better match and your father
agrees!" She was literally clapping her
hands with joy.

Lillian gasped, her head started to spin.
She thought she would be sick. She had to
sit down or she knew she would be. It was
what she feared. This had to be a
nightmare. Her father swore to her that her
marriage would be for love, not land or
politics. How could he do this to her? He
was just sitting there looking like a sheep
waiting for slaughter. Why was he not
saying something? Anything! He should be
telling her mother this was ridiculous,
insane, outlandish.

"Father?"

"Sweet Pea, I know this is difficult for you
to grasp right now…"

"Difficult!" She was approaching hysteria.

"Sweet pea, it's all so new to you right now, but I think you'll agree when you have time to sort it all out, that it would be a fine match, don't you pussycat?"

She couldn't believe her ears and just as she was about to disagree vehemently with her father's assessment of the situation, Lord Montfort opened the door as if he had been outside the entire time. He had probably been eavesdropping. He seemed just slimy enough to do such a thing. He lifted Lillian's hand and kissed it gently, and again, she thought she would be nauseated. He lifted her hair and kneeled down close enough so that only she could hear. She could smell his fetid breath and feel his offensive touch on her shoulder.

"I hear we will be wed soon, and you should count your lucky stars that I, Lord Simon Montfort, would even consider marrying you, the daughter of a Devorn, such a minor noble, barely noble at all I should say. I can state with certainty that I would not entertain the thought whatsoever if you did not please my, uh, randy side. I expect nothing short of complete obedience, considering how many political alliances your buffoon of a father is going to receive from me. Are we clear?" At that moment, he put his tongue in her ear and traveled down her cheek with his slimy tongue.

She felt his spittle on her face and would have slapped him but was sure her mother wouldn't have believed a word she had to say about the encounter, seeing as the lord had such a brilliant smile pasted on his hateful face.

Her mother was simply beaming, "Now isn't that nice, you two getting along so well already."

"Mother, may I be excused," Lillian said between clenched teeth.

"I suppose so, I'm sure you've had an exhausting evening. My little girl is all grown up, isn't she?"

Lillian ran up the stairs as fast as her gown would allow and washed her face until it stung, to get the filth of his spit off of her. She fell into bed and tried for sleep praying that what she had just experienced had been a nightmare and not real at all, or at least that her father would consider her feelings and change his mind. She finally found restless sleep with strange and frightening dreams, always with a dark and menacing figure lurking nearby. She awoke in a sweat in the middle of the night, unable or unwilling to fall back asleep. Her situation was unfathomable. She had never in her entire life thought she would be facing a fate as horrible as this one. She had believed in her father and his promise. How could he have betrayed her so, simply because of her mother's influence? She shouldn't be surprised. Circumstances of her mother winning out had taken place all of her life, but she didn't think it would happen again, especially in a situation this important, with a man this

hideous. She couldn't help herself as tears
streamed down her face. She must have
fallen asleep again because when she opened
her eyes the sun was shining through her
windows. The day was beginning and the
birds were chirping and it seemed the world
did not know it was ending. Indeed,
everything was just as it was last eve, all
the events unfortunately had *not* been a
terrible nightmare. It was all there for
her to remember in lurid clarity.

Chapter 3

The day began early for Eriik and his men
and as camp broke Sol had just started his
journey across the sky creating a blazing
spectacle. The men began their customary
preparations and the journey started as
quietly as the dew melts upon the knolls.
The sun glinted off their swords and shields
and they appeared something akin to ancient
gods crossing the wide expanse of the
English countryside, so strong, so full of
bravado. As the sun crept higher into the
sky they were well on their way to the
castle. As it arose out of the mist, they
knew what agony awaited the inhabitants, but
Eriik took no pleasure in it.

****

For Lillian, the day seemed like every other
day only for a few minutes, then she noticed
a strange amount of activity going on
downstairs, women screaming and people
scurrying around. *What in the world?* Was
everyone aware of her fate and just as
traumatized as she was? No, that was
ridiculous. The inhabitants of the castle
would probably think Lord Montfort was a
good match for her too. He was a wealthy
man, and after all, no one marries for love.
She used to think she would be one of the
lucky ones, until now. She dressed hurriedly
and flew downstairs, surprised that people
were not only scurrying around and screaming
but gathering weapons as well. Mothers were

taking their children to safety within the castle walls and farmers were coming from their homes in the fields into the safety of the fortress. Something very wrong was astir. She asked everyone running by what was happening, but no one would stop to explain. She called for her father but he was nowhere to be found. The huge turret doors were being closed by chains, operated by the strongest men. She had to find out what was wrong. Since no one would take the time to talk to her, she ran up the steps to the tower, the entire countryside at her feet. In the tower, what she saw was unbelievable and horrifying. Men, or at least she thought they were men, huge beings with shields and weapons, marching toward her father's land. As she stood transfixed, they reached a point and started making camp as if they belonged there. They looked more dangerous than anything she had ever seen in her life. *What did they want? Were they indeed threatening? It appeared that the answer to that question was yes.*

Lillian ran back downstairs. The castle looked to be in chaos, but as she looked closer, she noticed that everyone seemed to have a duty and they were going about it precisely. She continued to look for her father and noticed the sun was climbing into the sky when he and his men came out of the drawing room looking grim but earnest. *She would never feel the same about that room again after her encounter with the vile Lord Montfort.* They seemed intense, perhaps they had a plan. She certainly hoped it was a good one!

Frederick caught a glance of Lillian and
stopped to give her a hug and assure her
that their walls were high, strong, secure,
and would not be overrun. Lillian thought
her father knew everything, at least she
used to, and his comforting words made her
feel better. He told her to go and help the
other women with the chores, especially
heating the oil they would be pouring onto
the enemy's heads if they tried to scale the
walls. She felt even better after hearing
about the hot oil. How could the enemy make
any progress with hot oil raining down upon
their heads. Her father did know
everything. It was nice to have something
to occupy her mind and keep her busy. It
gave her less time to think. She ran off to
find Gertrude, their trusted housekeeper.

After all the preparations that could be
made *were* made, the castle settled into a
nervous waiting game. They really didn't
know what to do or expect next. This enemy
wasn't acting like any other they had ever
encountered. They didn't attempt to make
contact or storm the castle. They were
simply making camp and sleeping in shifts.
It made no sense. It was like they were on
a picnic. One man in the castle that caught
Lillian's attention was Lord Montfort,
whining and trying to buy himself passage
out of danger. He was screaming so all
could hear about how preposterous it was
that this ridiculous castle did not have an
escape route for the important nobles, such
as himself. All he wanted to do was run.
He was wretched. No one seemed to be taking
him seriously or help him escape though. The
thought of his hands on her flesh seemed

that much worse knowing what a coward he
was. She was sure if her mother knew her
thoughts she would say she was being a brat,
but she didn't really care what her mother
thought at this moment, or ever really. At
any rate, she would not worry about the
loathsome lord any more until this was over.

Chapter 4

Eriik and his men finished setting up camp.
They sharpened their swords and axes and
felled a good sized tree. All the branches
were stripped and it would become an
effective battering ram. This was the first
of several days before the siege would
begin. It was all a part of the plan Eriik
and his advisors had conceived.

He paced back and forth, north and south,
for the most part of the next few days. He
wanted to know each and every rock between
their camp and the bastion.

On many of these walks, he noticed a
particularly fetching sight in the tower. A
beautiful girl with long dark hair had
bewitched him for some reason and he never
got tired of staring at her. The sun would
catch the auburn highlights in her hair and
it would produce a fiery display for his
pleasure. Every time he caught himself
gazing at her, his crotch replied with a
tightening, uncomfortable feeling that he
didn't often feel without easy relief at
hand, but she was there, easy fodder for his
observation and he couldn't seem to stop
himself. Whenever he would see Bjorn
walking near he would tear himself away,
knowing full well how severely he would be
teased if Bjorn found out what he was up to.

Eriik and Bjorn would laugh as they spoke of
listening to the people in the castle

shouting and scurrying around as they
prepared for them, knowing full well they
were getting no rest. That was a good
thing. Tired warriors were sloppy warriors.

"This is rather fun, playing with them like
this Eriik, but I must admit to being itchy
to swing my sword."

"Oh, be patient my friend. The way they are
running around like geese, we can simply
wait around, knock on their door, and they
will be so tired, they'll open the gate and
offer us some ale."

They both guffawed.

"If you can be patient until the moon no
longer appears over the horizon in three
nights, it will all begin."

"Ah, the moon will be hidden and provide the
darkness we need. They will not be
expecting us and then we will pounce, like
the wolf."

Eriik winked, "That's the plan. Tell the
men to prepare for hot oil being launched
off the top of the wall raining down on our
heads. I think we would need to avoid that
if at all possible." He grinned. "When it
does come, tell the men to gather together
under their shields, forming a pod,
protecting themselves as much as possible.
When the time is right the archers will
strike with their arrows straight and true
while the others continue to batter the gate
with the ram. Spread the word!"

"Aye, brother." Brothers in arms they were, and had been as long as Eriik could remember, even as boys.

****

When the town nearby received the news that the fortress was under siege by a foreign army, a rescue party of sort showed up quite willing and able to provide encouragement and support, not for the castle, but for Eriik and his men. The rescue party consisted of some very talented ladies who knew their customers would be ripe for the picking for their special talents. There was a lot of money waiting to be made and the ladies were eager to please. The men were ready for the whores, and nary a complaint was made. Eriik had no objections as long as it didn't interfere with their fighting fitness when the time came. It was actually a delightful diversion from their daily life of swordplay and preparation, and the men reveled in it. They needed the respite after the long voyage and the tense standoff here. The girls sang and danced and soon their clothing ended up in complete disarray, sorely tempting the men until they started disappearing into the tents, more often than not with more than one man.

Bjorn, laughing and completely enjoying the festivities, looked at Eriik and prodded him, "Go on brother, join in, what are you waiting for? You're usually the first after such a long voyage. Ya going to make do with sloppy seconds, or worse?"

"After painting such a lovely picture, I'm really looking forward to it." He cocked his head with a smirk.

"Well, you can look at the stars all night and receive no loving, I'm staking my territory and getting some ass!" He strode to the fire with long even strides.

Eriik looked at the woman with long blonde hair who was gazing back at him with desire written all over her face, and she was very appealing, but for some reason he could only picture the sun dancing off sable tresses. This woman's skin was brown from the sun, and he could only see beautiful fair skin in his mind's eye. What in bloody hell was wrong with him?

He walked with ground eating strides over to the girl, took her arm, smiled his most charming smile, and practically stole her off her feet as he headed for his tent. He placed her on his robes and covered her with his massive form.

She was smiling. "You will be particularly fun," she said teasingly. "You're a handsome lad and I can see and feel you are endowed quite well. The money's the bait but I'm already looking forward to tussling with you a bit. I know you can't understand a word I'm saying but I bet you can understand this."

She parted her blouse and he could easily see her full and heavy breasts. They were also browned by the sun. Her nipples were large and erect and she squeezed them as she lifted one breast high enough so she could

lick her own nipple, already hardened by her
tongue seductively. He was taking in the
sight and his cock was strong, bulging,
hard, and throbbing. She was squirming
under him, parting his tunic to get a feel
of his impressive chest rippling with pure
muscle. She was grinding herself right on
target on his swollen flesh. She was ready
for him. What was he waiting for? All he
wanted to do was push himself inside to his
hilt, fill her completely and ram her until
his sublime release. By Thor, he couldn't
move! All he could think of was the lady in
the tower. He would ram himself into this
one and think about the sable strands of
silk he had been staring at for the past few
days. He couldn't understand why he was so
fixated on this particular girl when he
couldn't even really see her, just basically
a figure. A quite nice one, but just a
figure nonetheless. He suddenly looked at
this whore and stopped himself. *Why?* He
got up and backed away. He couldn't imagine
why he was doing such a thing. It wasn't as
if he had never found relief in the arms of
a prostitute before. She slithered over to
him and rubbed her crotch against his
swollen cock as her fingertips stroked his
chest. He grabbed her hands, looked into
her eyes and instead of saying something
seductive, he said in a controlled, but firm
voice, "I can indeed understand everything
you said and I tell you now, you need to
get out girl, go on now, do as I say." She
winced, gathered her clothing and ran out as
if the tent was on fire. After she was
outside, she looked back with what looked

like regret. Eriik would probably live to regret his actions as well.

The other men had no such problems. They were coupling with everything they could get their hands on, waiting in line at times. After getting finished with one girl, some of the men would go to another tent to take on another. They were having quite an enjoyable evening. They couldn't say much for the English warriors, but their whores were impressive.

Eriik was glad his men could burn off their energy and frustrations. They would need a release after these days of waiting and it would do them good when the time came for battle. He rested, tried to sleep but only the lady paraded through his head. He knew not if it was a dream or if he was wide awake. Nevertheless, he was wondering if he was losing his mind.

Chapter 5

The days in the castle went by and everyone
was on pins and needles. The talk was of
these heathens' plans, and non-stop
gossiping about the men themselves, mostly
of their leader, the tallest and most
muscular of these giants. With his long,
golden hair, he fought with a sword, axe,
javelin, and bow expertly. The men were
talking about his expertise with his weapons
and how to defeat him but their women spoke
of him in much different ways, usually
giggling and blushing. They knew he was
their enemy, but couldn't help themselves
when it came to his obvious physical
attributes. When their husbands came along,
their conversation changed to terror again,
their feelings being a little of both.
Lillian and all the young ladies of the
court were also terrified and fascinated
with him at the same time. Lillian couldn't
help herself when she ran up to the tower to
sneak a look at him when no one noticed. A
couple of times some of her ladies in
waiting accompanied her as they watched him
pace up and down the field and practice
weaponry with his men. As they stared
Lillian felt thrilling sensations that she
couldn't quite explain and realized that if
her mother knew, she would be locked in her
room for a week as punishment. It all
seemed so innocent up in the tower so far
beyond his reach. But sometimes she noticed
that he would be looking back at her and
could imagine their eyes locking even if it
was too far away to really know. She

thought perhaps she was imagining it, but some strange feelings would jolt her stomach and between her thighs and while Lillian had never had these particular sensations before, they were very disconcerting.

She really had no rationalization for such strange emotions and the tingling was not all that dreadful, so she decided to treat this like everything else she couldn't, or didn't want to explain, and place it in the back of her mind until another time.

Eriik, on the other hand couldn't stop thinking of the lady of the manor with the pale, beautiful skin, and the long dark locks. Surely it was because he had not had a woman in such a long time. *And whose fault was that?* Why else would he be focusing on this particular girl, this Saxon wench, probably not hardy enough to lay with him without swooning. What the hell was he thinking about lying with a Saxon girl anyway? He must pray to Thor to get his mind back on the siege, not burying himself in an English lady. He had plenty of time to bury himself between the thighs of a willing woman in Jaedon after he got home, the conquering hero. He had let the lady best him in one arena already, without so much as a skirmish. He had given his archers strict orders not to aim at her or her ladies when she visited the tower. What was her stupid father thinking, letting her put herself out in the open like that? Didn't he know she would be an easy target for an archer sneaking up on the castle unseen? Eriik's judgment had already been compromised by a beautiful woman. That had never happened before. He should let them take the shot and cripple the castle before the battle even began. He wasn't much for murdering young maidens anyway, he tried to convince himself. This would have to be the first and the last time he let this happen though. By the Gods, he promised himself. Mind over body, victory must be his goal.

It was time. The moon had almost completely disappeared. The sky appeared as a beautiful length of black velvet dotted with diamonds thrown up in the heavens in complete disarray. Eriik's men all knew this was the night. As the days had passed, the castle settled down at night and fewer men patrolled the walls. The castle was letting down their guard and that was what the Norsemen were waiting for as well. It inevitably happened after days and days of high alert when nothing occurred. The men walked as quietly as a predator stealing up on its prey, until they were at the walls, seemingly unnoticed. The men carrying the tree trunk were stealthy, even with such a heavy load; to them it was nothing, and they made absolutely no sound. It was all going according to plan. Eriik expected no less. Everything was dead quiet and the castle was calm until the entire building shook to its core with an explosive sound that awoke everyone inside with terror. They thought the world was coming to an end or possibly it was judgment day. Perhaps it was.

The battering ram crashed into the castle gates with such force that the ground shook. Birds took to the sky and animals in the fields ran for their lives. For quite awhile, the Saxons had no idea what was happening. After gathering their wits, they started for the oil, but it was not hot, and no one was up to heat it. This was beginning to look like a rout. The Saxons had never seen fighting like this. Were these mere men or demons from hell?

Eriik's men kept smashing into the heavy wooden gates, time after time. No one inside could imagine the strength it must take to move that tree again and again. As archers appeared on the walls, they flew their arrows and screams of pain radiated from the ground through the air. Eriik noticed men carrying buckets and he knew that this must be the oil.

He screamed out, "Form the pods!"

All the men formed the pods as the oil came rushing down the walls to fall on a solid wall of shields, hurting no Norseman. When the buckets were empty, the ramming continued. This went on all night and the next day and the gates were looking the worse for wear. After a full night and day of tireless work, Eriik called it and the men retired to their camp for food, rest, and to gather their dead. The English couldn't believe what strength it took to fight tirelessly all night and day with no food and barely any water. They couldn't help but wonder if these were mere men or something from another realm.

The next day proved to be the same as the last. By the end of the second day, the gates looked as if a small child could knock

them off their hinges. Eriik called the day
again and decided to give the castle an
ultimatum tomorrow at dawn. Unlike many of
his kinsmen, Eriik was not fond of killing
for no good reason, if he could achieve the
goal peacefully. Through the days of the
siege, his one failure was the girl, dammit.
He was expecting victory and already
dreading leaving her.

Damnation! Stop it. What in the name of
Thor was wrong with him? Enough! He
finally fell into a restless sleep with
thoughts of long russet silk falling in wave
after wave down a slender alluring back. He
awoke with a start. It was nearing dawn.

Chapter 6

The day awoke sunny. The air was as crisp
as a summer apple and Eriik breathed it in
deeply, almost being able to taste it. It
invigorated his senses and strengthened his
purpose.

The men were stirring and in barely a
moment, they were ready. They gathered
around him and started the walk in their
battle formation toward the castle. Eriik,
in front, stood firm.

"Lord of the Castle. Listen and live, you
and your people. Your fortress will not
stand another day. Submit to our demands
and your citadel will not be crushed, your
women will not be taken, your men will not
be beheaded and your castle will not be
occupied. Give us your treasure willingly
and go about your business in peace."

Lord Devorn appeared at the top of the wall,
looking sheepish as his voice shook, "Never,
as long as I live."

Eriik's voice was strong as he shrugged,
"I'm afraid Lord, that will not be long."

Eriik pointed to the fortress and the men
with the ram took their place. The battle
started again, but with pleasure, the
Norsemen noticed there was no oil showering
down upon them this day. The castle's
archers were still busy but it seemed each
day they were fewer and the Norsemen's
archers were still strong in number and aim.

Each time the ram struck, the gates groaned and shuttered. They were starting to open the slightest bit in the mid-section. It shouldn't be long now.

Inside the fortress, the able-bodied, fighting men, were armed and at the ready, just waiting now for the inevitable. Lillian stood at the top of the stairs and wept. She caught her father's eye as she started to descend the steps and she knew he was telling her not to come down under any circumstances. She obeyed.

The ram made its final surge and the gates crumpled. The Norseman exploded inside the walls of the fortress that all inside had thought would protect them and their families. It looked like a certain bloodbath but Eriik shouted in a full and strong voice, "Stop, everyone now!" For some reason, not only did his men honor the command but everyone in the castle did so as well. Perhaps they thought this could save their lives and most of them looked on with hope.

Eriik spoke again in a voice that was definitely in charge.

"Lord, do you see these warriors. They have stopped only because I commanded them to. They are ready to slaughter everyone in here. Is that what you want? Are your possessions worth your lives? I say nay!" Again and for the last time, I offer you your lives for the treasures of this fortress. Give them up willingly and we will return home and leave you in peace. This is fair!"

Lord Frederick hung his head, looked around at his people, terrified, and sorrowfully shook his head yes.

"Lord of the castle, I will hear your answer!"

Frederick looked at Eriik, Jarl of Jaedon in the eye and said quietly, "Yes, I agree to your terms."

A few of the English fighting men cried out, "No!"

Eriik raised his sword, "Don't tempt these men. They are the best warriors in the world. You will be slaughtered if you try us."

"I agree, I have no doubt of what you say." Frederick whispered. "Everyone will hand over their weapons." He gave a stern look, especially to the young, hardy men of the group.

The disarmament went on and Eriik and his men stayed, keeping the remaining men on watch outside, waiting. Any sign of a problem and they would swoop down on the fortress, bringing unbelievable horror upon the Saxons.

At the removal of every weapon and most of the treasure from the walls of the castle, being safely ensconced in the Viking camp, Lord Devorn asked Eriik, "Now will you remove your henchmen from my land?"

Eriik thought for several moments with thoughts of the lady running through his head. He knew he was about to insist on a very bad stipulation but he couldn't stop himself, "Only after we dine, here, tonight, with you and your family."

If a look could kill, the look on Lord Devorn's face would have struck Eriik Thorennson dead in his tracks.

"My God man, are you mad?"

"Possibly, but my demand still stands."

Frederick shook his head in defeat once more, "Give me your word that you will return to your camp immediately after, leave my land, and never return!"

Eriik lifted his eyebrow in a jaunty manner, "I will give you my word never to return to *your* land."

Eriik and all of his men laughed until their faces were red, "We will see you at dinner."

Some of the Norsemen returned to camp with the remainder of their plunder, congratulating themselves on their success and rested in shifts until time for dinner.

Bjorn looked at Eriik with a look of concern, "Why in Odin's name demand dinner with these Saxons?"

"I'm hungry." Eriik laughed.

Bjorn just shook his head. "This I will never understand."

"Well, they can't fight worth a damn, I thought maybe they could cook." He grinned.

As dusk drew near, Eriik and the men going to dinner approached the castle carefully. Some men had been guarding the bastion all day, but caution was always the way. They were shown in with forced hospitality and seated at a long table. The family arrived but he did not see the young lady he was looking for.

"Excuse me Lord, but I do not see everyone."

"I am here, my wife is here."

"I am looking for a particular young lady, fair of skin with long, dark hair. She looks out of the tower most days."

"My daughter?" Frederick exploded.

"Then, lord, your daughter is not here."

Frederick stuttered, "My good man…

"You are misinformed, my good man," he said sarcastically, "You'll find nothing good here, but for the last time, I asked you where your daughter is."

Frederick was so red in the face, the servants thought he might pass out of this world and on to the next, but through clenched teeth, he told Gertrude to fetch Lillian straight away.

Eriik told the servants to hold the food until the lady arrived. They looked to Frederick and he nodded.

When Lillian arrived, Eriik rose, none too gently moved the man beside him, who held himself like a strutting peacock, out of the way, and seated Lillian beside him.

She was so surprised that for a moment she thought she might trip and fall onto the table. *"What an entrance that would be,"* she thought to herself and smiled.

Eriik wondered what had put such a beautiful smile on her radiant face but didn't care much as long as she was here and alongside him for dinner. All the days he had watched her couldn't have prepared him for how stunning she was. He had imagined her so many times in his mind's eye but he was ill equipped for the real lady. He was caught quite unaware.

Lillian had watched this man so many times, but being next to him was something completely different. Watching him from afar was nothing to compare to seeing him up close. He was amazing. He was so tall and, mesmerizing. His thick, long, glorious hair framed his face, causing his blazing blue eyes to stand out even more. He had hard corded muscles over every inch of his body. Even the knights she had seen weren't his equal. His arms were so muscular that she couldn't imagine him being able to maneuver something as delicate as a fork. He had a band on each arm, outlining the taught muscles there. She was waiting for him to attack his food like an animal, but surprisingly, he ate quite civilized. She knew she was staring, but couldn't help herself. She knew she should hate this man with everything in her heart and soul but still could only manage to gawk at him.

Eriik knew she was staring at him because he was staring right back at her. He was sure she hated him with a blind fury, but all he could think about was the most alluring emerald green eyes he had ever seen and how it accented her beautiful long dark hair. It flowed down her back forcing one to notice how her back narrowed into a very graceful waist and shapely ass, just as he had imagined it would be, staring at her in the tower all those days. Oh yes, he would definitely like to bury himself in between those thighs. He could only imagine how beautiful they would be.

After a rather uncomfortable silence, they started an awkward conversation at first, which blossomed into quite an interesting one, which surprised Eriik. He couldn't imagine she would even talk to him. Lillian was a curious girl and couldn't get enough information about this gorgeous man from a land afar, especially how he learned to speak English, and Eriik couldn't get enough of telling her. After all, he could look at her while he was talking and that's exactly where he wanted to be and what he wanted to do. His men couldn't help but notice what an idiot Eriik was being over this Saxon wench. They couldn't believe it. Usually women threw themselves at *him*. He was the one who besotted the lasses and he could pick and choose, never interested very long after tossing up their skirts.

Eriik could tell that the man he moved was seething at his place at the table. Every time Lillian or Eriik would laugh, he could see the look of rage on his face as if he wanted to punch Eriik in the face. He would have loved to return the favor if he tried. Finally he guessed this peacock would have no more of it as he strode across the room and leaned in between Lillian and Eriik.

"Excuse me, sir, and I use the term loosely." He smiled an evil smile. "I am Lord Simon Montfort and you are cavorting around with my intended and I won't have it for another second!"

Eriik smiled widely, "Intended what?"

Lillian could hardly keep herself from smiling.

"You simpleton, intended wife. We are engaged to be wed."

Eriik's eyes glazed over and he seemed to slip into a trance for an instant before he spoke again. "Well that is indeed unfortunate."

"Why is that? What in the world business is it of yours?"

Eriik arose and raised his chalice, "Lord and Lady, I'm afraid I have one more demand and it is non-negotiable."

Frederick looked truly defeated, "What could you possible ask of us now?"

"Yes, just one more small requirement and you will be rid of me and my men forever.

He paused then stated sternly, "Your daughter must accompany me when we leave tomorrow."

He translated the demand for his men.

An audible gasp came from the residents in the castle along with his own men, the biggest from across the room from his best friend.

"What?" Bjorn swung around to face him. "What the hell do we need with a bawling princess? "By the gods, have you gone out of your bleeding mind? What can you possibly be thinking? I can't believe what I'm hearing."

Lillian couldn't either. Leave her home, her parents. Go with a complete stranger. Go where? To a foreign land among strange people and be a prisoner there? All this seemed impossible. Her father couldn't possibly allow this. He couldn't, he wouldn't! Why was life so difficult, especially for a woman. Why couldn't a woman decide for herself what she would do and where she would go. She bolted from the table without excusing herself and ran for her suite. If Mother was upset with her manners, then so be it.

Eriik watched her go and felt for her, but couldn't help himself. He wanted her. He would have her.

Frederick couldn't believe his ears. This heathen was going to take his little girl? He had been watching her all evening. She had talked with him, smiled at him, even laughed with him. But go away with him? He and his men had just laid siege to their castle and stolen most everything of value in it. That was intolerable! But the alternative, wed to Lord Montfort. Yes, his wife thought they needed him for political reasons but he knew that he was a cruel and manipulative man. What kind of man was this Norseman? Was he a demon, as everyone said?

The whole time he was lost in thought, this Lord Thorennson seemed to be waiting for something, watching him. Frederick came out of his reverie and noticed the Norseman looking at him.

"I understand that your men can and probably *will* kill everyone here at your command if I say no, and you will probably do just that, but I must tell you I cannot hand her over to a stranger, an enemy at that, to take her to a foreign land against her wishes. What do you say to that?"

"I do not have an answer. You must talk with her and at dawn tomorrow I will come for her. If you do not hand her over to me, my decision will be made then."

Eriik strode out with commanding strides and his men followed, amazed at what had just taken place and completely confused at their leader's actions. No one said a word.

Chapter 7

Frederick and Beatrice had been with
Lillian, talking and crying late into the
night. They had left her with her thoughts.
Lillian was still trying to put the pieces
together. She was a smart girl and she knew
what her choices were. She couldn't stay at
home and wait for the love of her life to
show up and they would live happily ever
after. That dream was shattered. Her
choices were too horrible to contemplate.
On one hand, she could say no to this
heathen, as Father called him, he said she
could. If she did so, would everyone in the
castle be slaughtered? She could never live
with herself if that happened. Besides, if
she didn't accompany him, he and his men
could slay everyone and take her anyway, or
kill her too. If that did not happen by
some miracle, then she would be Lady
Montfort, spending the rest of her life with
the loathsome, evil creature, Lord Montfort.
Her thoughts and *choices*, if you could call
it that, were whirling like a storm in her
head and she even started considering
running away, but that was no choice, it was
a nightmare. Run like a coward? Not on her
life, and it very well could be. "God
please show me the way!"

Her mind started flitting away from the
present into the future. The Norseman was
there, she was there. Could she find any
happiness with someone like him. He *was*
incredibly handsome. Oh how could she even
think about that now? Would there even be a

chance for any kind of life with him?
Wouldn't she be his prisoner? Really, did
she even know what he was like? He didn't
send his men into the castle to slaughter
everyone. He could have. That she knew for
sure. She had heard Father talking about
it. They did steal everything. What kind
of gentleman would do that? Not any kind of
gentleman she was used to, that was for
sure! What should she do?

****

At dawn, Eriik and his men were packed and
camp was broken. They approached the castle
much as they did many days ago, once again
in full battle gear, well prepared for
anything. Eriik spoke loudly and strongly.
Send the lady out. We are ready to leave!

There was no movement in the castle.

Eriik waited motionless.

Some of the men whispered to one another.
"Do we slay them all if they do not comply
or do we turn and leave?"

A lot of head shaking was going on.

Bjorn looked at Eriik questioningly, "Well,
what do we do?"

Eriik didn't budge, "Wait."

The castle was terrified. Lady Lillian
couldn't possibly be turned over to a band
of raiders, but what would become of them if
she was not?

Everyone was whispering and holding loved ones close when one by one all heads turned toward the stairs as Lillian slowly descended the stairway. She looked as if she were going to the gallows. Was she really going with them? Surely not! And just as everyone was guessing, she crossed the great room, hugged her father and said in a strong, loud voice, "Good bye, Father. Good bye, all. Step away from the gates please."

"Oh sweet pea!" The tears were coursing down his cheeks. Even Beatrice looked sad, probably upset about her lost political power. Lillian broke free and walked unfaltering toward Eriik without a whimper. The life she knew was over. A new life was beginning this day, and she prayed to God that she would not be wishing for death soon.

Eriik, even though he had made this a demand, was very surprised to see her walking straight for him, not wavering, not crying, as strong as any Norsewoman would have been. In a strange way, he was proud of her. When she reached him, he took her arm and with his entire army, walked quickly away, never looking back.

Chapter 8

Eriik led his men back to their camp on the beach and everyone started busying themselves for the night and the journey to come, everyone that is, except Lillian and the whores, who had followed behind. Lillian had never felt more uncomfortable in her entire life. The girls were talking amongst themselves, making bawdy comments about the men, trading uncouth stories about the nights they had spent with them, and Lillian was turning a brilliant shade of red. When one of the girls noticed her blushing, she put her arms around Lillian's shoulders and said loudly enough for most everyone to hear, "Don't worry dearie, you'll have your turn soon enough with the big one. I'd even bet you're a virgin too. Oh my, that should be a night to remember. Tell you what girlie, I'd be glad to trade places with ya, well not the virgin part. Don't think I could pull that off. But I wouldn't mind havin' a go at that one, eh ladies?" All the women laughed and Lillian hid her face in her cloak.

Lillian was not only embarrassed, but terrified, and not for the first time that day.

She sat in the same place, unmoving until Eriik approached with some food and water and said unemotionally, "Eat"…which she did. Her stomach had been feeling none too well but after eating the surprisingly good fare, she started to feel a little better. She

guessed she would stay there through the
night as it seemed she was the only one
without shelter, but before she could even
finish that thought, Eriik came walking over
to her with his usual long strides and she
came to a different conclusion just by the
look on his handsome face. Her conclusion
seemed to be correct. He took her by the
hand and swept her into his arms as if she
were nothing but a small child. She thought
about resisting but decided that would be
utterly absurd, considering his size and
strength. He would do what he would.

He set her down inside his tent and she
stood straight and tall. She would not cower
or beg. She would stand up to him and be
her father's daughter in every way, strong
and unfaltering. She looked him straight in
the eye, "Will you be raping me tonight?"

Eriik appreciated her directness, her
straight spine and strong attitude. He also
appreciated her full breasts, those wondrous
emerald eyes and long dark hair. By Thor,
how he wanted to caress her nipples and lave
them with his tongue. Instead, he looked
unaffected and said simply, "No. Wash up
and get ready for sleep. Tomorrow will be a
day like you've never had before and it will
be arduous. You will need every minute of
sleep and every ounce of energy you have.
You will sleep in my robes. You'll be safe.
A vessel of water is in the basin in the
corner. Use it quickly so we can retire."
She was so astonished, she could barely
move, until he looked back, "Move!"

Eriik was taking off his clothes, all of his clothes. She looked away as quickly as she could. When she was finished at the basin, he was lying down, naked! She didn't mean to look again but simply could not help herself. He was on his back with his hand over his eyes. She couldn't tell if he was already asleep or not. She would have been surprised to know how wide awake he really was. Her eyes slowly traveled down his magnificent body, from the splendid muscles on his arms and chest to, oh my, the very male part of him that she couldn't take her eyes off, even though she was chastising herself the entire time. What was wrong with her? That part of the male anatomy was certainly a mystery to her and it had not been of any interest at all until this minute. Now she couldn't take her eyes off it. It brought to mind the knight's stallions. Oh my, that thought made her blush as she turned quickly away and splashed more water on her face. After drying off again, she sat down in the corner.

Eriik looked up, "I said you'll be sleeping in my robes tonight. Did I not make myself clear?"

"I will not sleep in the same bed with you. It's not, well it's just not proper."

"Not proper? What in Odin's name are you talking about girl?"

"You are not my husband and therefore I will not be sleeping in the same bed as you."

"Well let me put it to you this way lady. You will either come over here by your own volition or I will truss you up and bring you over here by force. Your choice." It would be better for you if you came yourself." He looked at her as if she were an unruly child.

She decided she would be better off doing as he said. She tip toed to his make-shift bed and lay down as far away from him as she could get.

"Will you be sleeping in your traveling clothes?" he muttered.

"Yes indeed."

"You will wish tomorrow that you had not. None of my business."

He put his hands over his eyes again as if he were going to sleep.

Lillian, with all her might, still could not stop herself from staring when she thought he was asleep.

Eriik had never been more wide awake and very aware of her perusal of him, and it took every ounce of control he possessed to keep from becoming very thick and very hard. He knew he could not continue to do that for very much longer, so he turned away from her and let his imagination run amok. At every turn, when he thought of her creamy breasts, shapely waist and derriere, he grew heavy and hard. He was in abject misery. Why did he not take her? That's what she was expecting after all. That was not his way,

he wanted her eager, wet and willing,
moaning and calling his name when he spilled
his seed inside her. Yes, that's what would
make his release worthwhile. He could have
any woman he wanted just to ram himself
into. He didn't understand exactly why he
wanted this woman to be different, but he
did, and at that moment he decided he would
set out to win her into his robes willingly.
After quite awhile his cock settled down and
so did he. Sleep was filled with emerald
eyes and burnished silk. When he awoke,
remembering the wonderful dreams of her, he
wondered if he would ever be able to keep
his mind on something else? By Thor that
was a good question.

Chapter 9

Camp broke early and the small boats were
loaded and re-loaded time and again to get
all the men and treasure back to the
longships. The prostitutes were left behind
in spite of a few of their pleadings to come
along. Lillian was hoping that perhaps she
too would be left behind, but that was not
to be. She was astonished to feel the huge
vessel take so easily to the sea as the huge
oars sliced through the water and the men
taxed their muscles. She couldn't believe
how easily they managed the heavy oars in
the water. She gasped as the icy sea water
came arcing through the air and hit her like
a slap in the face when the oars dipped into
the water and then rose high into the sky.
She was fascinated, but quite aware that
this would probably be a very uncomfortable
voyage. She couldn't believe that with
every stroke of the oars she was moving
farther and farther away from her home and
her family. Tears sprang to her eyes, but
with strength and purpose, she stopped them
immediately. Without realizing it, she sat
a little straighter and appeared a little
more resolved. Every time she thought she
would surely break down, the thought of the
repugnant Lord Montfort made her feel just
the slightest bit better.

The days were infinite, dreary, and wet. It
was hard for Lillian to imagine ever being
warm and dry again. At night she would join
Eriik in his robes and every night, true to
his word, he left her alone, turned over and

went to sleep, leaving her in peace. What
was to become of her though? She couldn't
figure out what her place was in the scheme
of things, his demanding her to accompany
him. Why? Some things are better left to
God, she guessed. She certainly hoped God
was close at hand and had not abandoned her.

One night, she woke up to find Eriik facing
her back with his broad arm thrown
carelessly across her waist. She turned
gently over to face him and couldn't help
but notice how immensely masculine he was.
He was sleeping so peacefully, she didn't
have the heart to wake him. What in the
world was wrong with her? He had seized her
home, ransacked it and kidnapped her. Why
was she having gentle feelings for him? It
infuriated her. Was she mad at him or
herself? Oh! She turned over violently,
shaking Eriik awake harshly.

He had been having a sensual dream about
making love to Lillian on a beautiful grassy
mountain. She was wet and open for him to
slip inside and he took her uninhibited and
brought her to the peak of ecstasy. His
cock was full and demanding and she took
every inch of him and cried out for more,
then…nothing. He was jarred awake none too
gently.

The men were astir. She asked Eriik what
was going on and he said they had sent out
the ravens and they had not returned, which
meant they should be expecting land soon.
This news brought two emotions within
Lillian, fear and pleasure. She couldn't be
happier to get off this damn boat, but the

thought of being in a foreign land where no
one except Eriik even spoke her language.
Oh wait, Eriik had told her there were some
English priests there, one of which lived in
his household. That was something, after
all. Would the townspeople be hostile?
Again, what was to be would be. She
silently prayed for help and strength to
persevere. It was the next day when the men
started shouting about seagulls and
according to Eriik, that meant they were
very close. They should be landing sometime
tomorrow. Thank the Lord, this would be the
last night on this god forsaken ship. But
then…

Chapter 10

They could hear the horns informing everyone in the village they had been spotted. It looked to Lillian as if everybody had shown up on the dock to welcome their men back home, some of which were not returning to their loved ones alive. Her hands were shaking and she could not stop them to save her life. Unexpectedly, Eriik grabbed one of Lillian's hands and gave it a squeeze. This little gesture from Eriik meant the world to Lillian even if she wouldn't admit it, even to herself. Eriik helped Lillian off the boat and showed her a place to sit while the unloading and the greeting of kinsmen took place. After awhile she was very glad she had a place to sit because this arrival and unloading was taking an eternity. She leaned back against a rock and became quite pensive, reflecting about all that had happened to her in a mere week. She noticed Eriik walking toward her and again found herself thinking how he was so tall and muscularly built and how absolutely male he was. She couldn't help the chills that went racing down her spine but chastised herself for feeling that way about her abductor. He reached her and stated firmly, "Time to go home."

"Home? My home is in England!"

"Not anymore sweet."

"Don't you dare call me that."

"I'll call you what I like."

With that, he grabbed her hand and they
started off, pulling a cart behind. One of
his kinsmen had provided it for Eriik so he
could take all his plunder home. Anger
could hardly describe what Lillian was
feeling. He called her Father's pet name
and now was pulling all her family's
treasure behind him. *Oh*!

By the time they finally arrived at his
home, she was too tired to feel much of
anything, even anger. She would try to fire
herself up again later. His dwelling was
quite large, considering she was expecting a
grass hut with livestock grazing inside. It
was cut literally out of the side of a
mountain. The work was quite skillful.
There were magical looking signs and
ornamentation sculpted on much of the front
of the abode. It was very beautiful. At
least it would have been had she been in any
other mood. Even so, she couldn't help but
notice the expert craftsmanship.

He opened the door for her and as she
entered, she actually felt quite cozy and
deemed herself a traitor not only to her
family, but to England as a whole for such
feelings. Would she never be able to feel
like herself again? She seemed to always be
fighting within and it was wearing her out.
The beautiful wall hangings from the
ceilings were magnificent. The great room
had a table that looked as if it could seat
a hundred guests for dinner. The staircase
was carved with more foreign but beautiful
symbols. She didn't know if they meant
something or if they were just for
appearances.

Eriik showed her to a bedchamber and it was
exquisite with two huge windows from ceiling
to floor with window hangings even more
ornate than in the great room. It even held
a tub. Oh, good lord, how long had it been
since she had the luxury of a real bath?
She was overwhelmed. She was chastising
herself for being so impressed, but couldn't
help herself from looking forward to staying
in such a stunning suite.

Eriik said, "Do you think you could be
comfortable here?"

"Oh my, yes, well, uh, it's not home, but…"

He started to smile but caught himself
before she saw it.

"I know, but we can't change that now can
we?"

"At any rate, welcome to my chamber."

She whirled around so fast she became dizzy,
"Oh no, if you think I am going to be your
mistress, you are sadly mistaken!"

"Lillian, you have shared my bed now for
days and I've kept my word."

"Yes but that was in horrible conditions,
not in a nice, soft bed in a lovely room."

"Well, how about if you stay here just long
enough for a nice, hot bath?"

To her utter amazement he started a fire,
then ordered several servants to bring hot
water for her bath. Heaven on earth, a hot
bath after that hell of a voyage. She

couldn't help but smile at him and at that moment, upon seeing her smile, it took all that was in him not to rush over, take her in his arms and ravish her with his mouth and his body.

Instead, he said, "Well, I'll leave you to it, then."

Haltingly, she replied, "Thank you, Eriik, uh Lord Thorennson."

"Please, Eriik."

He had to leave in a hurry before he changed his mind and kissed her with the lust that was rampaging through him. He was a strong man and he could control every aspect of his body, but at this moment his flesh was getting the best of him and he could not control his damnable cock. It was hard, uncomfortable, and throbbing with pain. He wanted to slide into her until he couldn't push any further. What was wrong with him? He couldn't ever remember wanting a woman this much. It made him weak and he could not tolerate being weak. He had to have her, and when he wanted something, by Thor, he got it!

He stomped down the stairs and out of the house, straight to the tavern to join his men and kinsmen for a drink, or many drinks, and some well-earned celebration.

When he arrived at the tavern, the revelry was well on its way. Everyone was having a good time and as he entered, the entire tavern jumped up, got him a drink and

toasted their success, attributing most of
it to him.

"Ah no my friends, thanks to us all and to
the gods!"

The party was amusing and he was glad he
came, when he felt a soft touch on the back
of his neck, caressing him. He knew before
he turned around who he would find. One of
the tavern wenches, Jorunn was behind him
with a very saucy look on her face. She was
tall and blonde with her long hair pulled
together in one long braid falling down the
center of her back. Eriik knew how she felt
about him and was certain of her intentions.
He would usually be more than happy to
oblige, but for some reason, she didn't seem
quite as alluring as she always had before.
His body however was traitorous. He could
feel the heavy, full feeling flowing through
his groin again. She saw it too and was
rather pleased with herself. She sat on his
lap and discreetly rubbed his crotch,
chafing herself against the hardness that
was straining for release. They laughed and
drank and after a few pints, Jorunn said
seductively, "Let's go upstairs handsome."

"I'm right behind you."

No one even noticed them as they climbed the
stairs to a small bed chamber. Jorunn
closed the door and pulled her outer
clothing over her head. She had nothing on
underneath. Her breasts were naked for
Eriik's hungry gaze, but he stood
motionless. She teased him by touching her
own breasts and then pushed his shirt aside

to caress his chest. She was getting the
desired affect but he was still making no
move to touch her. She was taken aback
because normally, he took her immediately
and their lovemaking was wild. *He's
probably tired after his long trip*. She lay
on the bed and spread her legs so he could
see for himself what treasure was within.
Her fair curls were wet with anticipation
and she rubbed herself and licked her lips
in an erotic dance of allure.

Eriik was so hard he was miserable. What
was he waiting for? He couldn't figure it
out and either could she, but he seemed
stuck to the floor.

Jorunn was getting frustrated as she stalked
Eriik like a cat playing with its prey.

"Darling, I can see you are hard and ready
for me, what are you waiting for? Perhaps
you would like me to help you out of those
breeches?"

She pulled his shirt off his back and
stroked his impressive chest, while grasping
his swollen cock through his trousers. She
chafed her breasts across his chest causing
her nipples to harden with desire. As she
continued to tease him, she loosened his
pants, and as he sprang forth, Eriik
couldn't help but sigh with relief. Before
she could bend down to put her berry stained
lips on him, he suddenly pulled back,
fastened his pants, grabbed his shirt, and
backed out the door. Jorunn couldn't
believe what she had just witnessed.

Perhaps Eriik caught a sickness from the foreign land.

Without a word to anyone, Eriik struck out for home. All he wanted to do was see Lillian. Well, that's not *all* he wanted to do.

Chapter 11

As he reached his land, he slowed his stride and thought about what he needed to do. This was an impossible situation. He had a woman that he wanted to take but couldn't and all the women he could have, but didn't want. A never ending ridiculous circle.

As he entered his bedchamber, Lillian was in her bedclothes lying in bed with her back to the door. She seemed to be asleep. He came in, stripped down, and climbed into bed. As Lillian felt his body beside her, it was as if he were the devil himself; she flew out of bed and shuddered. Noticing his nakedness, she turned and cried, "My lord, I believe I made myself perfectly clear. If you wish to sleep in your chamber, please have the servants make up another for me."

He was drunk, frustrated, and generally disagreeable, "I'll do no such thing. Get your ass in this bed on your own or I'll hog tie you."

"Excuse my indelicate language, sir, but like hell you will."

Eriik leaped across the bed in one motion, grabbed Lillian's hands and brought her flying into his arms, sitting her down upon his naked lap. She started to struggle, but soon realized it was futile and besides it was causing quite a difference in Eriik's particular body part that she had been focusing on of late.

"Now, would you like to sleep or be tied?"

She turned her nose up and said nothing.

"I'm going to ask you one more time and believe me Lillian when I tell you, one more time!"

She spit in his face. She was furious!

He was more than enraged!

He threw her over his shoulder, her fighting him every step of the way, to no avail, as he pulled the cord from the window hangings. He tied one end of the cord around her waist and attached the other end to his wrist.

"You had your choice, lady," he hissed. "Sleep well."

****

Each night was like the last. He would arrive at his bedchamber, he would ask her the same question and Lillian would turn up her nose and shake her head. He would tie her to him and she would go to sleep, or try to. Eriik also had a difficult time sleeping as he lay with his back to her, seething. He was vehement that she would lie with him on her own accord or she would be tethered to him every damn night.

However, night after night he would hear her weeping softly and felt like such a bastard, but the thought of her sleeping anywhere but beside him was unthinkable.

Lillian now was not only a prisoner by day, confined to his bedchamber but truly a

prisoner by night as well, in his bed.
Wasn't that what she had been afraid of,
being a prisoner? But was he really the one
imprisoning her, or was she doing this to
herself out of sheer stubbornness? Either
way, this was a mockery. She could not go
on much longer. Perhaps she should just
open the window and throw herself to her
death. Taking one's own life was an
unforgiveable sin and even if she had the
courage in this life, she certainly didn't
have the courage to spend eternity in hell.
Although right now she felt like she was
already there.

Alright, she said to herself sensibly, *what
must I do*? *I cannot endure this situation
any longer.*

She had the entire day to ponder this very
important question, and so she did. Besides
Eriik, she was completely alone and
increasingly finding it unpleasant. The
days were infinitely long, as she languished
away in his bedchamber, with nothing to do
but nap and longingly look out the window.
She wasn't sure what to do about it, after
all, no one but Eriik could speak to her
even if she *were* allowed out of the room.
She had no one to talk to and nothing to do
and even if she did, she would have been too
embarrassed. Thinking of Eriik, she
couldn't help but picture his magnificent
body, the fine muscles, and dammit, that
strange feeling in her stomach started again
with a weird quivering feeling. She needed
to calm down a bit. She got up to snoop
around his bed chamber and found a cabinet
full of liquor. She had never been allowed

to drink before except wine at dinner. She
felt absolutely decadent. Everything was in
beautiful decanters, so she didn't really
know what she was picking, but she chose the
one that smelled the best. There were two
goblets by the decanters. For some reason,
those two goblets pricked her. She imagined
he had company in this room all the time.
He had taken his clothes off in front of her
with no modesty at all, not that he had any
reason to be modest. But still, she was
sure he had taken his clothes off plenty of
times with many women. There goes that
prickly feeling again. Completely
ridiculous! She drank the dark, warm liquid
and it burned going down, but it felt good.
She thought and drank, and thought and drank
until the quivering stopped and there was a
nice warmth flowing through her body. She
felt good. Her head was spinning a bit, but
it was fun. She laughed to herself and
tried to walk to the bed but fell, giggling.
She heard him come through the gate
screaming about something and gulped the
remainder of the drink down, fast.

Chapter 12

He had had a particularly long, hot,
frustrating day of swordplay with Bjorn, but
couldn't sweat his randyness away. He had
gone longer without a woman than ever
before, and why? What the hell was he doing
anyway. Bjorn was right. He had lost his
mind.

He was thinking about his present sleeping
arrangement and all of a sudden he thought,
"*Dammit*! Something had to change, and "It's
going to change soon!" he shouted to the
heavens.

No one seemed too shocked. They all knew he
was besotted with this Saxon woman and
believed, from the whispers of the chamber
maids, that he was getting nothing in his
robes.

Eriik climbed the stairs to his bedchamber
and without knocking threw the door open
with such force, it smashed into the wall,
startling Lillian.

"I'm so sorry my lady, didn't mean to
frighten you. Let's just say I've had
somewhat of a frustrating day," he said
sarcastically.

"My lord, I thought the devil himself had
come."

"Perhaps you are correct."

Eriik smiled and just for an instant, so did
Lillian. Damn, there was that smile again.

It could tame a wild animal and it certainly was having that effect on him.

Eriik softened for just a minute and said sincerely, "Lillian, aside from the fact that I took you from your family, and nothing can be done about that now. You have to accept it. I've been kind to you, yes?"

"Kind?"

He walked so close to her that he could feel her breath on his face. He was a little taken aback to smell brandy but put the thought aside.

She wanted to come closer to the musky, male scent of him, but made herself pull back.

He gently put his rough fingers on her soft cheek, then without her permission, touched her lips with his own. He felt her intake of breath and for an instant, he thought she would accept his kiss, but she didn't. It was simply a soft, gentle kiss, nothing more. He backed off, strode out of the room and slammed the door, not to return that night.

Her heart was racing and she was unsteady on her feet. She should be angry, terrified, anything but what she actually felt, excited. How could she be excited about this pagan putting his hands on her and his lips touching hers? But the fact was…if she was honest with herself, and she always tried to be, she was stirred, and worse than that, she was eager for it to happen again. By the saints, what was wrong with her? She

was raised to be a good girl! She had been
kissed before but it certainly had not felt
like that. What did it mean? She needed to
settle down. She would make sure he never
know she was anything but repelled. All she
could think of was hard muscles and oh no,
she would not think of that. When he was
kissing her, he was pressed up against her
body and she could feel it hard and
demanding and as disgusted as she was with
herself, it pleased her. Shouldn't that
have repulsed her? She knew nothing at this
moment except her relationship with Eriik
was a hoax and she was the one preserving
it. That realization was quite profound.
She was finally being honest with herself,
if nothing else.

Chapter 13

That night was the first night she spent
completely alone since she was forced to
leave her home. She should be delighted,
but she wasn't. She felt abandoned and
forsaken. She paced back and forth, hoping
Eriik would show up. What in God's name was
wrong with her? She wanted her captor with
her? She told herself that she needed to
think about her current situation and come
up with some answers as it was unfathomable
to consider leaving it this way for any
length of time. Honestly, leaving her home
was awful, well leaving her father was. Her
mother was more than happy to turn her over
to that horrid Lord Montfort for prestige
and political gain. She would probably be
his wife by now and that thought brought
bile to the back of her throat. How did she
really feel about Eriik? And how did he
really feel about her? Was she his slave,
his servant, his mistress? The chamber
maids whispered when they were in her
presence, but she couldn't speak the
language so she could only surmise what they
were saying about her. She would have been
surprised to find out they were talking
about the fact that the master had never
brought another woman into his private bed
chamber before. There had been many women
come in and out of the manor, but always
bedded the master in another chamber.

Lillian thought they were giggling about
their sleeping together, well they *were*
sleeping together, but…

She knew that Lord Montfort was a dreadfully
cruel and evil man and deep in her heart she
would rather be right where she was than
anywhere near him. She actually admitted it
to herself for the first time since she
walked out of her home and away with Eriik.
Now she had to have the guts to set her
course and put it into action.

The next day she decided some liquid courage
was in order. She made her way to the
cabinet with the pretty decanters and idled
away the afternoon drinking and trying to be
brutally honest with herself. For the most
part, she was.

Eriik had had enough of lying next to
Lillian tied to his body, weeping. He was
going to ask her one more time to be
civilized and if she refused, he was going
to move her to another room. As much as he
dreaded it, he couldn't take one more night
of this absurdity.

He burst into the room expecting to find,
well he didn't quite know what, but a drunk
Lillian was not one of them. She was trying
to get to the bed unsuccessfully so he
picked her up, laid her down, and was
completely taken by surprise when she pulled
his lips to hers and kissed him, much more
passionately than he had kissed her the
other evening. He knew she was drunk and he
should stop, but he couldn't quite make
himself.

She, on the other hand was feeling emotions
she never thought possible. Her breasts
felt tight and she had strong bristly

sensations between her thighs. Her nipples
hardened and were tingling. She wanted to
feel his chest, the muscles there. In fact,
she wanted to feel him everywhere, yes
everywhere. She knew he was hard and
throbbing, that was evident and it was
exhilarating. She did not want to stop.
She parted his shirt and caressed his chest,
splitting her time between his chest and his
handsome face. Then, she did something she
never thought she would do in a million
years, she reached down and felt the bulge
in his breeches. She heard him gasp and
then he took her hands strongly and held
them away from him. She was so
disappointed, she couldn't believe it.

"No, I want you."

"You're drunk. Dammit! I want you when
you're sober and know what you're doing."

"I know exacterly what I'm doing."

"Exacterly? I don't think so."

He kept her hands in his, put her head on
his chest and lulled her to sleep. He had
been through many battles and other
hardships, but had never done anything this
difficult. He wanted her more than his very
life, but he wanted her on his own terms,
when she was in her right mind. This gave
him hope. At least on some level, perhaps
just physically, she wanted him. Isn't that
all he needed?

Chapter 14

The next day she awoke with the sunshine
awash through the large, lavish windows.
She started to get up when a pain in her
head stopped her short. Oh, she remembered
the whiskey, but not much else. Eriik was
gone and she was still dressed. That was a
good sign. She kept telling herself that
she wanted nothing to do with him but her
body was telling her something completely
different and she knew it deep down, but
nothing in the world would let her admit
that she wanted a physical relationship with
the man that kidnapped and took her away
from her home and family.

She freshened up, changed into a fresh
frock, went to the door as usual, and to her
surprise found it unlocked, so she carefully
proceeded downstairs. If she was to start a
life here, she decided she should begin
today. Apparently Eriik agreed. As she
took one step after another, she could feel
the stares and felt as awkward as a one
legged goose. She straightened her back,
lifted her chin, and said, "Good morning,
all." She expected no return greeting as no
one except Eriik spoke English. She did not
see him anywhere but when she heard, "Good
morning my lady," she whirled around with a
start. She was astonished to see a priest
bowing to her in a most grand fashion. She
couldn't believe her good fortune. Hadn't
Eriik mentioned this priest before? All the

days past ran together in a fog. At any
rate, here he was and she was most grateful.
She ran down the rest of the stairs in a
flurry of skirts and brought him up from his
knees to shake his hand furiously.

"Oh my I'm so delighted to see you. I was
afraid I was the only one in this strange
land to speak English, well except for
Eriik, I mean Lord Thorennson.

"No my lady, there are several of us here
and I live in this household. Permit me to
introduce myself, I'm Oliver. I've been
told to be at your service at all times as
you wish."

"Thank the lord!"

"Yes, indeed." He looked towards the heavens
and crossed himself.

Matter of fact, he stated, "The first order
of business I would think is to get you some
breakfast and then settle down and start
some sort of routine for you. Don't tell
Master Thorennson, but I heard him tell
everyone in the household to treat you like
the lady of the house."

"Really?"

"Oh, yes Lady Devorn."

"I, uh, can't imagine that. That truly
stuns me." At his look of trepidation, she
continued, "But I won't breathe a word of
it."

"Thank you lady."

They continued on to the large kjokken, the kitchen, where several women were working diligently. He introduced her to the woman who seemed to be the boss. Her name was Geirhild. She made Lillian an exceptional breakfast and then they started in on the task of inserting Lillian into the routine of the household. He conferred with Geirhild, not only the boss of the kjokken, but the principal keeper of the entire house, and she agreed.

"Oliver, how have you become so strong with this strange language? Have you been here long?"

"No, my lady, I had been on a missionary journey long ago and learned this, among other languages."

She pondered for a moment, "I would hate to inconvenience you, but do you think you could teach me?"

"No inconvenience at all, it would be my pleasure Lady Devorn."

＊＊＊＊

That night in the bedchamber, Eriik looked deeply into Lillians green emerald eyes, "Lillian, please tell me you'll sleep here with me unrestrained. I'll ask you one more time, tied or free?"

There was a long silence, then in a tiny voice, she whispered, "Free."

He was not only surprised but relieved.

"Aye, get some sleep then." He smiled, put his arm around her waist and for the first time in weeks, slept a deep and sound sleep.

This nightly arrangement went on for weeks. Not that she would admit to it, but his presence, his arm about her waist, snuggled up to her back, became very comfortable. She couldn't believe the way she felt about him and experienced quite a lot of guilt because of it, but feelings were something one could not control. More thinking on the subject might be in order.

The house settled into a routine with Lillian becoming a part of it. She was allowed anywhere on the property now and each day she became a little less nervous. Eriik gave her a beautiful little mare she named Molly and they became the best of friends. Oliver was teaching her Eriik's language and she had a real flare for it. She amazed Eriik each day with her progress. It pleased her when he would comment on how proud he was of her. The household of Thorennson was taking notice of how the lord and lady were getting along.

Ventures were taken more and more into town. At first it was not pleasant, as she received stares of condemnation and anger. However as time went on, the townspeople became friendlier, as Lillian greeted them and carried on small conversations in their language. It impressed them.

In the bedchamber, Eriik's arm around her, or her arm or head resting on his chest became a way of life, and it was very

comforting. She continued to fool herself
into believing that she was his hostage, but
if she were to be objective, she would know
that she was falling more and more into his
web of seduction. When he was near, her
heart would flutter, her blood would race in
her veins, and most traitorous of all, she
would feel a tingling between her thighs and
her nipples would feel tight. If he knew
that, she would be mortified!

Eriik did know however. He could tell how
flustered she became when he was near. What
she didn't know was every time they were
near each other, he was like a raging bull.
His groin would ache and his cock would
become full, heavy, and practically burst
from his breeches. He wondered if she was
ever the wiser when he always excused
himself in her presence and not return for
awhile. This could not go on much longer.
He had had just about enough and decided
tonight things needed to change. With his
mind made up, the damn thing started growing
hard again, and with a curse, he headed
outside to walk it off. He would have liked
to ride, but in his condition, that would
have been far too painful.

For Eriik, dinner seemed to take forever.
As soon as he had eaten his fill, he excused
himself, took Lillian's hand and walked with
her hurriedly up the stairs, slamming the
door in his wake. Lillian was a bit
troubled by Eriik's behavior and knew
something was amiss by the aggravated look
on his gorgeous face.

"Suddenly pleasant again, he commented airily, "Would you like a warm after-dinner brandy Lillian?"

That seemed a little strange, he had never offered her brandy before but it did seem enticing.

"Yes, that sounds lovely."

Eriik put the brandy goblets close to the flames of the fireplace until his hands couldn't stand the heat any longer, then handed one to her. She tasted the fiery liquid and it was sweet on her lips.

"This is quite good, thank you."

The look in his eye was disconcerting but mesmerizing at the same time. "Yes, quite good."

He put his drink down and walked slowly to Lillian as close as possible without touching her, bent down and gently licked the brandy off her lips.

She felt the breath in her lungs expel as she took in the scent of him. He smelled of the sweet liquor. She felt heady when he put his lips on hers and gave her a sweet kiss that she wanted desperately to return, but would not give in to her desire. She stood completely still at first, then backed up a step. Eriik put his large hands on her small shoulders and kissed her again more urgently this time.

"Lord Thorennson, this is not proper. I must demand that you stop."

"You, demand? I don't think you are in any position to be making demands of me. I'm sorry you don't feel this is proper, but right at this moment in time, I really don't give a damn."

"Eriik, don't."

"Lillian, you are putting up this false face for some stupid propriety that doesn't mean a thing here, when you know good and well that's not how you really feel."

She whirled around with her back to him. "I don't know what you're talking about."

In truth, she didn't want him to see her breasts heaving with desire. The result was to give Eriik the chance to retrieve his knife and slit the tiny hand crafted buttons all the way down her slender back, and as they danced upon the floor, she clutched the bodice of her dress desperately, but Eriik grasped it and jerked it to the floor. Her dress slipped down her legs to reveal nothing but her delicate chemise.

Lillian could hardly breathe.

She stood completely still clenching her chemise with all her might. She was trembling but couldn't seem to move away. Eriik thought she was trembling from fear and would have been shocked to know it was from something completely different, excitement and perhaps even anticipation. Eriik swept her hair aside and caressed the nape of her neck and shoulders with his fingertips. Shivers cascaded down her back as his lips gently replaced his fingers as he kissed her neck and ran his fingers through the silk of her hair. She knew she should walk away and demand that he stop but couldn't force herself to move away from his touch. He picked her up gently and placed her on the bed and there was no mistaking the look of pure lust escaping from his blue orbs as he looked deeply into her emerald ones. Lillian wanted to touch him but held herself still out of pride. She put her hands up to Eriik's chest, in her mind to push him away, but the feel of strong, steely muscle stayed her hands and she jerked them away. Eriik brushed his lips against hers in a tender kiss and although Lillian felt so many emotions she compelled herself to remain still. As Eriik continued his gentle assault on her tender lips, he attentively teased her thighs with his fingers. Her supple legs felt like satin and he couldn't get enough. When he parted them the slightest bit and caressed her inner thighs, she couldn't help but sigh. He once again turned his attention to her beautiful mouth and parted her lips just the slightest bit while touching her tongue with his. An electric shock ran through her body and scorched her. A chill went flowing up her spine. She was wet and tingling and couldn't put two words together to make a thought. Somewhere in the back of her mind, she knew she should be turning away, but she couldn't resist any longer and she didn't want to. This was pure pleasure, pure heat. He started a little swordplay with her tongue, and that, plus feeling his fabulous, sculpted body, was her undoing. She made a small gesture. She tentatively started

kissing him back. This touching of tongues,
she had never done before and even though
she thought she should be disgusted, she was
anything but. His tongue felt like velvet
in her mouth and he tasted like brandy. Her
body was touching him from head to toe and
it felt like the room was spinning. He
kissed her mouth, her cheeks, her neck and
down to her bountiful breasts. He laved the
top of her creamy mounds with his tongue,
cupped her soft breasts in his calloused
hands, and she sighed softly. As he was
busy kissing her décolletage, he ran his
fingers up to the sweet nectar of the
triangle between her thighs. She gasped
only for a second because as she threw her
head back in ecstasy, she was giving him his
way with her breasts and neck, and he took
full advantage.

As he pushed the delicate material away so
he could view her unspoiled beauty, he
brushed her nipples softly with his thumb
until the pink buds were hard and wanting
for more.

To his utter surprise, she parted his shirt,
almost tearing it off his chest. She
caressed his muscular chest with tiny
swirling motions and kissed his nipples.
She ran her fingers through his golden hair
and looked deeply into his sea blue eyes.

*How long she had wanted to do that, she
thought.*

He was crazy with desire as was she. As
much as he did not want to do this, he
pushed her slightly away from him, looked at

her straight in the eye and said softly,
"This must be your choice as well as mine."

She lowered her lashes and nodded.

His groin was throbbing, and after her
assent he couldn't go back now if Odin
himself was at the front gates.

He pulled the strings of her chemise and she
was bare to his hungry eyes as he brought
her back into his arms. There she was,
flawless, more than he had imagined night
after night, with her beautiful hair spun
like silk, waiting for him to take her. He
had a strong surge of emotion, which was so
unlike him. He hurriedly separated himself
from his clothing and heard her gasp.

"What is it sweet?"

Calling her sweet this time was pleasing to
her ears.

She looked away blushing furiously.

He waited.

"Please don't stare at me like that." She
felt completely exposed.

"I'm sorry, but it's indeed a most wondrous
pleasure!"

He held her, stroking her naked body with
his hands and his tongue. She was writhing
and moaning, but before he went any further,
he asked her again.

She blushed again, "You are…"

"Tell me."

"You are so…" in a tiny little voice, she finished, "big."

Eriik couldn't contain himself as he roared with laughter.

"Oh my sweet Lillian. I promise you, I will take you so you will feel little pain. Do you trust me?"

She nodded and he started his expert manipulations of her tender body once more. He held her hands above her head and kissed her tenderly, opening her mouth with his tongue, following the curve of her neck to the valley between her breasts. With his fingers, he traced the curve of her hip and parted her thighs and with gentle strokes, he traveled up her inner thigh, touching the most tender place of all, the wet russet curls between her legs. She moaned and Eriik thought he might go out of his mind with this tantalizing torture. Her eyes were closed as her head tossed back and forth. He explored the outside of the damp triangle, then ever so tenderly parted her and placed one finger inside. He almost lost control when he felt how wet and tight she was. He stopped for a moment to gain some rule over his rampaging lust before continuing. He promised her little pain, and he was going to keep that promise. He could feel her tightening and relaxing around his finger as he explored the wonders inside. As she made little sounds of pleasure, he gently inserted another finger to get her ready. He stopped again, then continued his domination of her body. He knew she was a virgin, so he would need to

prepare her well. He slowly lowered himself
onto her, carefully. He kissed her deeply,
urgently, placing his cock at her opening
and it strained for her. He chafed the area
around the apex of her thighs and felt how
slick she was as she strained and gyrated
around him, wanting him. She spread her
legs wide open to receive him, welcoming him
as he groaned with pleasure. He kissed her
breasts and stomach, neck and face and as
subtly as he could, slid into her just a
little. Her eyes flew open and her face
froze. She was a maiden no longer, he had
taken it for all time. This was a defining
moment in her life and nothing would ever be
the same for her again. He looked into her
emerald green pools and was drowning there.

He was right, the pain passed and something
else took over. This feeling of need. She
didn't know what exactly, but she wanted to
hold him inside her until it became clear.
Her body wanted something, ached for
something and she gasped for air. She
spread her legs wider and with her body,
motioned for him to enter more fully. He
looked at her questioningly but complied.
He filled her up so perfectly. Oh God, this
wasn't nearly as painful. She almost felt
complete, but still lacked… she didn't know,
she couldn't know, it was illusive. She
felt she needed to move somehow, to achieve
something. She wanted him to move with her,
but he stayed motionless.

He looked at her, "I'm not all the way
inside you yet. Her eyes were open wide.
He slid in even more. Her eyes were
enormous now. Oh yes, he was huge! He was

inside all the way now and completely still,
and rightly so. It took just a few minutes
for her body to adjust this time. It didn't
take any time though for her to adjust to
him lying on top of her, feeling his
bountiful weight felt wonderful. She loved
it. She ran her fingernails down his
strapping back and held his buttocks in her
hands. As she got used to the fullness
inside, it felt good! It felt right! When
she started to flex her muscles around him,
he smiled and started to move, slowly at
first then gradually faster, but controlled.
She couldn't believe the beautiful ache,
tiny bursts of sensations she could never
describe in any language. Tingling and
slick, she started to move with him stroke
for stroke, striving for that illusive
something. She knew it was to be found in
his body. She thought he was waiting for it
too, but she felt so inadequate. She knew
not what she was doing. She was moving her
legs and flexing her throbbing muscles
around him, a sensual dance of the ages.
Her body felt like it was on a cliff and
needed to fall but teetered on the edge for
what seemed an eternity. It felt fabulous
but she sensed she would fall at any moment,
but never did, when all of a sudden, her
body erupted into tiny explosions and
brilliant colors burst behind her eyes. She
screamed out, not being able to stop. Wave
after wave gripped her and she couldn't get
enough of his body inside of her. This was
the most astonishing feeling. She had tried
to imagine a man making love to her before
but the imaginings fell flat compared to
this incredible experience. After the

spasms that were washing over her wave after
wave started to erode and she was still,
Eriik looked at her, started to push into
her again, making sure he was not hurting
her and in a few moments, his face
tightened, there was a look resembling a
grimace on his face, he groaned like an
angry bear, all his muscles flexed, hard,
then just as suddenly as it began, he
relaxed. He was breathing hard and kissing
her lips and neck. He had a radiant smile
on his face, making him more attractive than
ever. He would have liked to stay coiled
inside of her forever but he was sure she
would be sore tomorrow, so he gently pulled
out and rolled over, bringing her next to
him with his cock cuddled up to her ass.
They were both still, simply breathing and
holding each other. Lillian was smiling,
trying to feel guilty about what had
transpired between them. She should, after
all, they were not married, but after what
she had just experienced, guilt was the last
emotion she could conjure up. She was glad,
however, they were here and not in England.

Eriik was feeling everything. He had never
taken a woman that equaled what he had just
felt. He'd tossed up his fair share of
skirts in his time, but nothing like that,
and she was a virgin, completely
inexperienced. He had expected nothing.

He stroked her hair and she rubbed his
fingers. They said not a word but
contentedly fell into a deep sleep holding
each other serenely.

Catherine Sharp
Viking's Desire81

Chapter 15

The next morning, their lovemaking was plain
for all to see and even though it had been
the most remarkable night Lillian had ever
spent, she was embarrassed for the chamber
maids to see the blood smears. It was proof
that she had lost her virginity, not in the
marriage bed with a loving husband who had
sworn to love, honor, and cherish her, but
by her treacherous body that could not stay
pure around Eriik, who she would love to
accuse of rape, but that would be the most
immense falsehood of her lifetime. She
couldn't do that to him or herself. She
would stand up to the stares of ridicule and
come what may, act the part of, well, his
mistress. That's what she was after all.
One of her dreads, and again, she had done
it to herself. He did not force himself on
her, he even asked her. By God, she looked
him right in the eye and gave him
permission. Without a marriage, lord
without even an admission of love or
fidelity. Oh she tried to feel unclean and
all she could feel was giddy. She was so
tired of trying to be someone she was not.
Honestly she felt wonderful after last
night. She straightened herself up, held
her head high, and went on about her day.
She yearned for this man she had wantonly
given herself to and if she was just a
mistress for him, then damn it, what would
be would be. Isn't that what she always
said? I'll think no more about it today.
Last night was too incredible to ruin it
with incriminations today. She could not

wipe the smile off her face. It felt
splendid.

After that first tumultuous lovemaking, each
night when Eriik came to their bedchamber,
the same wonderful ritual followed, and even
though the first few times, Lillian tried a
few feeble attempts to resist, she soon
decided it was futile to try. She was
besotted by his charm, fine body, and
incredible skills at lovemaking. That
thought pricked her a bit as she knew very
well how he had acquired those skills,
practice.

Every day that passed, she became more
proficient at her household chores and the
Norse language, not to mention her own
boudoir skills. They often spoke Norse at
dinner and she could easily carry on
conversations with the inhabitants of the
house. She tried to control herself but
knew deep down that she was falling in love
with Eriik. She felt comfortable and even
light-headed at times when he would hold
her, stroke her hair, and especially when he
made love to her.

She watched him at his battle games during
the day, his great muscles flexing with
exertion, as he swung his sword or axe, the
tiny rivulets of sweat running down his
back. Every time an opponent swung at him,
she had to cover her eyes. She couldn't
believe they were only practicing with those
dangerous weapons. One hit and a limb could
be easily severed. But each day they went
on and no one seemed to be wounded. What a
sight Eriik was as he usually practiced

without a shirt in the summer and she was
mesmerized by the play of each set of
muscles as he used his sword, axe, and bow.
Every day she was aghast at herself at how
she would feel as she stared at him. Her
hands would sweat, her breasts would
tighten, her thighs would tingle, and she
would fantasize about him atop her in bed as
his powerful frame would press intimately
into her welcoming flesh. She would
chastise herself but deep down she knew it
was to no avail. He was a sight to behold
and she couldn't get enough. She was also
proud when he beat his opponent, as usual.
*"What was she to do though? Did Eriik feel
anything for her? Well lust of course.
That she knew only too well. Obviously she
felt the same for him.*

He had never mentioned marriage or whatever
they do here to seal a relationship between
a man and woman. She didn't really know a
lot about it. He seemed content and the
people around him accepted her, at least she
assumed they did. It was all so confusing."

Well there was nothing she could do about it
right now so she decided to go about her
business, and quit worrying about it.

$$****$$

Eriik had been talking to Bjorn about
Lillian that very day, about his position as
Jarl and his feelings for Lillian.

"I love her. That's the way of it. But
does she love me back and even if she does,
can I make it legal between her and I, being
the Jarl?"

"Brother, I would say you can do any damn thing ya want, being the Jarl," he laughed and slapped Eriik on the back.

"I'm expected to join with a woman to expand our land and our coffers, yes? Political dung as it is."

"Is that what you really want to do, brother?"

"I just told you it is not!"

"Then pray to Odin, grow some balls, and join with the woman you love," he rode away yelling back, "but tonight we drink!"

Eriik laughed, thinking that was a fine idea.

Before he left for the tavern, he pulled Renouf aside, "Listen my friend, do me a good turn my man."

"Anything my lord."

"Do some snooping around and see if I were to join with Lady Lillian if she would be accepted as my wife."

"Oh lord, congratulations."

"Not a word to anyone, I'm depending on your discretion."

"Yes, yes my lord, you can count on me."

Eriik certainly hoped so, and went on his way to drink his problems away that evening. Unusual for him though, he went inside first and informed Lillian of his plans. "What has become of me, he thought, and chided himself for becoming so domestic."

In so many ways though, it felt good and he was hopeful the people would welcome Lillian with open arms. He certainly had. Really, he had fallen in love with her the first time he had spotted her with her long, flowing hair in the tower. It was fated by the gods, he was sure of it.

At the tavern, he was in his cups and happy to be with friends and neighbors, but anxious to go home and lay atop his beautiful Lillian. Odin, could he ever get enough of her? He was beginning to think the answer to that question was no. All the other women in his life lost their appeal soon after the coupling was over. He guessed that was the difference between loving and lusting. Lusting and sex was nice but making love *with* your love was another thing entirely. It must be blessed by the gods themselves. As he was thinking of loving and coupling his steps became faster and his cock became thicker. *"That damn thing has a mind of its own,"* he thought. And its mind is always on Lillian.

He raced for home and up the stairs to find Lillian sitting up in bed waiting for him. The loveliest sight he could imagine. He was in his cups, yes, but nothing would prevent him from making love to her tonight. He dropped every bit of clothing right there on the floor and noticed her smile as she lowered her lashes. He had a notion that she liked his body and it made him even harder. His cock was full and heavy and reached for his navel. He walked to her side of the bed and gently opened her nightclothes and put them aside. There could be no one comelier. He intended to make this last. The liquor was already wearing off and his rioting lust was taking over. He swept a lock of hair off her face as he bent down to take her lips in a demanding kiss and her tongue entwined with his. The play of their tongues made him want to take her right then, but he took a deep breath and controlled himself just as he did in battle when the enemy tried to provoke him to attack before it was time. She wasn't helping either as she writhed upon the bed and spread her legs for him, but he was determined. He had plans for the lovely Lillian tonight. He broke loose from her tasty lips and traveled down to her inviting breasts to give them the attention they deserved. She grabbed his hair and wrapped her legs around his waist, placing her just at the right place for his pulsating cock to enter her, and it was difficult to wait, especially when he felt her moisture. But he just let his manhood twitch and tease her womanhood until she was thrashing in exquisite torture. He continued his journey down her breathtaking body to her belly where he kissed and played with his tongue.

"Take me Eriik, I'm ready."

"But I'm not sweet."

"Oh God."

"Sorry, darling, you keep forgetting, I'm just a man," he laughed and she tickled him playfully.

He started to concentrate again on her. As his head went down between her legs, she gasped and grabbed his head between her hands and momentarily stopped him. He held her hands in one of his and touched the wetness there with his tongue. She looked shocked and tried to object but only a moan of bliss could be heard. He softly ran his tongue over her curls and finally he entered her. She tossed her head to and fro. He knew her sweet release would come. She had never imagined that such exquisite feelings even existed. The fruit of her essence clutched his tongue and her muscles pulsated with excruciating need. Shards of the heavens started to rain down on her as she trembled. She scraped his back and squeezed with all her might. She was falling and falling and he was the only one who could catch her and then it broke, everything broke and she whimpered, then groaned, then screamed with delight. This continued on and on and he could feel her flexing around his tongue until she fell limp and exhausted and he kissed her legs and belly and lay beside her as she continued to pulse and quiver. It was quite a long time before she could speak.

"Eriik, what in the world?"

"Did you not care for it my lady?"

She blushed furiously and rolled into his arms. "You must be out of your mind. It

was, was, I can't find words but you have
not found your release yet.

"I will, don't worry. The night is still
young."

She cuddled up to him and in a few minutes,
he started to embrace her breasts slowly and
lick her nipples with just the tip of his
tongue. He traced a line down her belly to
her lovely legs as he opened them.

She couldn't believe it but not only was she
still wet but she was ready to take him. A
smile lit up her radiant face.

"Eriik, my God."

"I keep telling you, I'm only a man, my
lady."

"I'm not so sure of that my lord!" she
laughed

He parted her again and stroked her with his
finger until she was moaning with desire and
then with one quick motion, Eriik pulled her
over and she was atop him, straddling his
huge cock.

"Eriik, you will surely impale me."

"Slowly, Lillian. Let me hold you. I'm
going to lower you down little by little
until you take me in."

And that's what he did. Slowly and little
by little, he lowered her down onto him
stopping while she adjusted until she
completely held his entire length inside her
body. She enveloped him completely. She

touched her fingers where their bodies
joined and smiled a wicked smile. In this
position, he felt bigger than ever, but
after remaining still for a few minutes, she
was used to it and it felt glorious. She
swung back and put her hands on Eriik's
knees and started slowly to rise up slowly
and place herself back down around him.
Eriik was beside himself with pleasure. She
was full of him in so many ways, physically
and emotionally.

Oh God she loved this man. Her heart welled
up with emotion and she decided then and
there that this was good. There could be
nothing wrong when everything felt this
right. She bent down to his face and looked
into his deep blue eyes and kissed his
forehead and his lips gently. She parted
his lips with her tongue and he met her with
his. The kiss deepened and the strokes of
their lovemaking increased. She couldn't
believe it, but the edge was coming into
view again and she was straining with her
legs, tightening around his cock so she
could achieve the fall. It was right in her
grasp. It was close, so close. Then the
heavens opened up and she was falling, oh so
wonderfully. Falling, falling. She screamed
out and then he bellowed and they fell to
earth, twisted together as one, their hearts
beating as one. Never again would either
feel whole without the other. She stayed
connected to him, inside of her, laying on
his massive chest, holding him close to her
and he was holding her as well. This was
the apex, the peak. Neither spoke for a few
minutes, he was stroking her hair and she
was caressing his chest. Reluctantly she

separated from him but they held each other, talking about nothing, anything, everything.

"Eriik I know you think of Bjorn as part of your family but is your true family gone?"

"Aye, my mother died in childbirth with me. I was told she was beautiful and gentle. My father was a fierce warrior, taken to Valhalla fast and straight, bravely in battle as he went raiding. Valhalla is our heaven. Any warrior killed in battle is taken there, shown the way by our goddess, Freya."

Lillian couldn't help her curiosity, "Were you and your father close?"

"No. He was too busy drinking, coupling, and raiding to pay too much attention to me. I was left on my own from an early age." His tone had become bitter.

"Eriik, I'm so sorry. Well, it seems you did quite well on your own." She meant it as a compliment and saw that Eriik took it as such. "It sounds a bit like my mother, but for very different reasons." She looked wistful.

"You had no loving relationship with her? Why?"

"She was too busy trying to acquire riches, land, and political power to have time for me except as a pawn, so that was the reason for the foul Lord Montfort being my betrothed." She laughed sarcastically.

"I knew you could never have loved that pitiful excuse for a man, did ya now?"

"Oh bless the lord, no. He is a despicable and evil man, but my mother convinced my father that she was doing the right thing, as she always did."

"Then I saved you." He grinned from ear to ear.

"Oh, you, you, arrogant ass!" She couldn't help but laugh.

He laughed too, but in a more serious tone added, "Aye, little one, I know the pain of missing the love of a parent, or both," he said under his breath.

"My father made up for it though, he spoiled me terribly."

"So that's why you're a spoiled brat, is it now?"

She started to sputter, but before she could get another word in, he kissed her with a scalding kiss, silencing her, if only temporarily. His body started to react, as it always did. It indeed had a mind of its own. After they made sweet, gentle love again, flesh against flesh, they lay holding each other silently. There was nothing to say, just feel. They fell asleep woven in each other's arms.

Chapter 16

One particularly nice afternoon, Lillian
decided to take Molly out for a ride. She
had the groom saddle her and off they went.
She came to the same crossroads she rode to
every time and decided that today she would
be a bit more adventurous and take the road
untraveled. This trail was definitely more
interesting, with strange plant life and the
high mountains in the background, but after
awhile, she began to wonder if she had
chosen well. The ground brush was beginning
to thicken and the trail had become nothing
more than a thin passage between the thick
copse of trees and thickets. This woodland
was very dense and she was beginning to be
apprehensive. She decided the only thing to
do was turn around and go back to the
crossroads. She tried something new and it
was not the right choice. So, she turned
Molly around and started back the way they
came. Or was it the way they came?
Everything looked exactly the same. She
tried to find the sun but the dense timbers
and the clouds blocked it out and the day
had become quite dreary in this dense
undergrowth. She rode until she felt quite
certain she had come far enough to find the
fork in the trail and when it had not come
into view, she became concerned that she was
riding in a big circle. Why in the world
had she decided to go into unfamiliar
territory by herself? Sometimes her choices
were complete idiocy and this seemed to be
one of them. Well no time for feminine
vapors, she must get herself out of this.

She yelled for help a couple of times and it echoed throughout the valley but no one answered. All of a sudden out of nowhere Molly reared up, unseating Lillian, turned and ran away. Molly was never out of control. What in the world? Lillian was thrown up against a tree and the breath was knocked right out of her. For a few minutes she couldn't move. She started to explore her body for injuries and decided nothing was broken, at least she hoped not. She got up with the help of the tree behind her and hugged it for a few minutes. What a dilemma. She had no idea how to get home, and no way to do so. She started off so slowly it would take her an eternity. She still couldn't figure out why Molly had acted so crazily. After a couple of steps, the why was answered. She came to a dead stop as she found herself at a precipice, looking over a steep cliff, the edge covered completely with thick brush and logs. She never saw it, but Molly did. Without Molly's astute sense, they both would have found their deaths. Now to get herself out of there.

$$****$$

As the afternoon waned, dinner was getting underway and there was no sign of Lillian, Eriik started pacing and raging to the gods. Did she try to run away? Where in hell would she try to run to? Was she hurt? She was unfamiliar with these forests. She could have very easily run off a cliff. Why did he allow her to ride off by herself? That was a mistake he would not make again. His mind made up, he took a few men and rode off in search of her. As each mile went by, his trepidation grew, and he swore to the gods and to himself that if he ever felt her in his arms again, he would tell her his feelings. Fear stabbed Eriik in the heart as he saw Molly running straight for them, her saddle empty. Everyone looked at Eriik with sympathy in their eyes. He growled, "Don't look at me that way, she's fine. Now let's find her!"

"Aye." Everyone put their swords to the sky and rode hell bent.

Chapter 17

As the sun dipped lower in the sky and
Lillian could hear the cries of wolves, she
became more frightened by the minute. Why
had she been so foolish to go off by herself
on a path she was unfamiliar with? Surely
Eriik would notice she was not home and come
looking for her. Home. How strange that
sounded, but it felt right. She felt at
home with Eriik now. Right now was
certainly not the time to be visiting that
particular issue. How was she going to stay
alive until he found her? Was he familiar
with this area? She started yelling his
name with no response. All she could hear
were the howls of the wolf pack and it
sounded closer. She was cold and sore and
she was scared to death.

Lillian continued to scream Eriik's name
hoping he was near enough to hear her urgent
call. She didn't know whether she should
stay in one place or try to find the fork in
the road. Wandering around in this dense
forest would most likely be quite dangerous
and she felt like she would be going around
in circles anyway. What if she had to spend
the night here? Perhaps she should at least
try to find some shelter before it became
completely dark. She looked around for an
overhang that would provide some sort of
protection, hoping with all her might she
would not need it. She knew in her heart
that Eriik was out looking for her right
now. It was just a matter of him being able

to find her in the midst of all this
woodland.

She set out slowly, not wanting to make any
more bad decisions, when out of nowhere, she
felt something grabbing her leg, taking her
off her feet. Had a wolf snuck up on her
and now she was his dinner?

"Good eve miss, now what a nice surprise,
finding a pretty little wench way out here
this time of the evening."

Lillian was staring into the face of a man
with long, unkempt hair looking every bit
the brigand she would imagine a criminal
would look like, and even though she was
grateful it was not a wolf licking his
chops, she was not the least bit at ease.

"Really sir, there was no reason to trip
me."

"Well couldn't be real sure what was out
here. Sure didn't expect a pretty lady ta
be wandering around out in these woods all
by herself."
"You see sir, my horse threw me and I'm
trying to find my way home. I would be
truly appreciative if you could assist me."

"Well I might be persuaded. Pleased to meet
you my lady. Rolf, come out and see what I
found."

An equally disheveled man with yellowed
teeth, more missing than not, appeared and
Lillian became even more concerned, "Eriik,
I'm over here," she shouted at the top of
her voice. "You see I'm waiting for my

husband to arrive. I'm sure he'll reward you for finding me and making sure I'm safe while we wait."

"Oh I'm sure we'll get our reward, but I don't hear nobody out looking for ya." He got so close she could smell the stale liquor on his breath and something else that reeked but she couldn't quite put her finger on exactly what it was.

Rolf came around and took Lillian's hand and she thought he was going to help her up, but instead, he held her down.

"What, what are doing?"

"Where are my manners? I didn't introduce myself. I'm Olav and this is Rolf and we're going to become real good friends tonight, uh until your husband gets here, that is." They both laughed.

"I swear, my husband is looking for me at this moment. He is the Jarl of Jaedon, Eriik Thorennson. If you harm me, I don't want to even think what he'll do to you."

"The Jarl, you say? What a little liar. He's not even married. I think we're gonna have a real good time tonight and you'll be the center attraction, don't ya think so Rolf?"

Rolf laughed again and tore Lilllian's bodice from her shoulder to her waist while holding her hands above her head.

She screamed as loud as she could but seemingly to no avail.

Olav held her legs apart with his own and started to undo his breeches with a leering grin on his grimy face.

"Hey, by the look of this wench's underthings, we got us a real highborn here. I never had me a real highborn before, have you Rolf?" Rolf snickered and shook his head no.

Lilllian was horrified, screaming and crying but fearing that there was no one to hear her and worse, no one to save her.

***

Eriik and his men held their torches high trying to see Molly's tracks but it was getting increasingly difficult to see much of anything in the darkness. They were doing fine until they found tracks leading off the path, then the forest seemed to crowd in around them. As they rode in the tangled mass of dense thicket, Eriik knew the men thought this was hopeless, a woman alone out here with the wolves and no weapon. He couldn't think of such a thing happening to his Lillian. What he wouldn't admit to many people was staring him straight in the face. He was hopelessly in love with her and if something happened, he would be inconsolable. His heart was thundering as he spurred Kriger, his war horse, on faster. He had Molly running up ahead and he was hoping she could find Lillian before the wolves did. Molly started to make twists and turns and Eriik didn't know whether she was taking them on a wild goose chase or knew where Lillian was, but followed her nonetheless. After a few moments, he heard a faint noise. He couldn't make it out at first, but then he could swear he was hearing a scream. Bjorn looked at him, "I hear her! I hear her! The horse has found her!"

"Thank the gods! Lillian, we're coming!" He bellowed in the loudest battle voice he could summon. After a few minutes he could hear her screams and crying plainly. The men spurred their horses on to as great a speed as possible in the dense copse. They had no idea what Lillian was facing. It didn't sound like wolves, but more like the human variety of predator. Eriik rode like he never had before, prodding Kriger on. It sounded like Lillian's life was very much in danger. When Eriik came upon the sight of Lillian being held down while a brute was pulling his trousers down to rape her, he couldn't believe the emotions he felt. He jumped off his horse before Kriger had actually come to a complete stop, grabbed Olav away from Lillian and smashed his head into a tree trunk so hard, it was amazing the man's head didn't split in two. If Bjorn hadn't stopped him, Eriik might have made that a reality. As Rolf saw this, he let Lillian go and raised his hands in defeat. Eriik spared both their lives, even though it took all the self-control he could manage. As he picked Lillian up, he shielded her in his arms, wrapping his cloak around her. She hid her face in his shoulder, but she was no longer crying tears of fear, but tears of joy. She had never felt so safe.

Eriik was sure these two were the cause of all the misdeeds going on of late, "I suppose these are the thieves that have been causing havoc on the farms over the ridge. Bjorn, can you take a few men and throw them in the oubliette. I imagine if they have any family, they will sentence them to death, but they will be the ones to dole out the punishment. If they forfeit the obligation, I shall be honored to do so in their stead. Thank you brothers. I know this was a lot to ask coming out here in the middle of nowhere and I thank you for myself as well as Lillian."

"Yes, thank you all," Lillian turned to all the men with a tearful but grateful gaze.

"Home then," Eriik shouted with relief.

Eriik would not let Lillian ride Molly home, insisting on holding her in front of him, and Kriger carried two home instead of one. He didn't want her to notice how thick and hard he had become, having her so close to him, especially after all she had endured that night. He was so thankful she was alright, he couldn't control his body's reaction. But at this moment he couldn't be responsible for trying to hold his reactions at bay. Lillian was safe and in his arms, where if he had his way, she would stay for all time.

After finally entering their bedchamber, Eriik embraced Lillian with a gentleness she thought was impossible considering his huge, imposing frame, and she was touched. She loved him and started to say the words a

hundred times but they stuck in her throat
and were never heard.

Eriik also needed to voice his love but it
remained unsaid. Why were those words so
hard for him? He stroked her smooth cheek
with his fingers and touched her lips with
his gently. He had intended to do no more
that night even though he wanted her so much
to open for him as a rose bud opens for the
morning sun so he could taste the sweet
elixir of her delightful body. She tasted
so sweet it was difficult not to stop. His
body was telling him to remove her tattered
clothes and slide inside of her but he
commanded himself not to. She had been
through quite an ordeal tonight and he was
doubtful she would want him tonight. He
would leave her alone, simply holding her
through the night. That would be enough.
He kissed her sweetly but to his surprise,
she responded in kind, kissing him back
ardently.

"My sweet, you've been through so much
tonight, are you sure?"

She wanted him as much as he wanted her,
"I'm never been more sure of anything in my
life."

He took his cloak from her shoulders and let
the torn bodice fall away so he could taste
the creamy flesh of her perfect breasts as
he laved his tongue across the pink buds of
her nipples. They hardened to his touch and
she moaned with desire. She helped him take
off the remainder of her riding habit as
well as his tunic so the only clothing left

between them was her delicate chemise and his trousers. She could see the huge bulge where his cock was straining for her and she suddenly decided to be daring and reached to free him of his breeches so she could grasp him, and was excited when she felt the velvety texture, so hard inside and so smooth outside. Eriik thought he would come apart but took a deep breath and as she was exploring that part of his body which she was not all that familiar with yet, he removed her chemise and she was naked for his hungry eyes. What a feast she was. Her gorgeous dark hair falling in wave after wave down her shoulders to her waist, and her unblemished thighs seemingly waiting for him to part and slide between them as nature always intended. He picked Lillian up, gently placing her on the bed. He wanted this moment to last forever but knew he didn't have the patience. He placed himself atop her, ran his thumb gently across her breast lightly and then entered her slowly and tenderly until he heard an intake of breath.

"Am I hurting you sweet?"

"No, you feel wonderful inside of me."

Hearing those words spurred him on as he continued until he was inside of her to his hilt. She reached down to feel where the female part of her met the male part of him and he brought his head down to meet her fiery lips while her tongue swept his mouth hard and wanting. She tightened her muscles time and again, she knew the ecstasy that was waiting, and she was almost there, but she stopped, she wanted to feel him fully first.

"Eriik, I want you to let go."

"Don't tease me sweet. I can't hold on much longer."

"I know. I want to see your face when you find your release. Please."

"Oh by the gods!" His strokes became faster and harder and as his face tightened and he screamed what sounded like an oath in Norse, she knew his seed was spilling into her. It was the most amazing feeling she had ever experienced and then she closed her eyes and let herself find the cliff and began to fall.

The next morning came and went with no words of love, but each promising themselves that it would come sooner than later and were sated completely in the arms of the other.

Chapter 18

The previous evening, before the uproar with
Lillian, Eriik had received word from Renouf
that the people would support Lillian as his
wife. She had won them over with her bright
smile, her grasp of their language and her
sweet disposition. With that, his path was
steady, an after dinner stroll, the three
very important words, and a proposal with
his grandmother's ring. He was so excited,
he could hardly wait. He informed the
chamber maids of some special instructions
he wanted to be carried out in his suite
tonight while dinner was being served. They
giggled until a steely gaze put them running
about their business once more.

A breathless Oliver came running through the
door with exciting news, *at least for him*,
Eriik thought. A band of traveling
missionaries had arrived in town to spread
the word of their god, and trade silk and
spices. Would it be with Eriik's favor to
invite them to dine at Thorennson Manor
tonight?

"I suppose so but I will not be able to
honor them with my presence into the late
evening as I have a very pressing
engagement." As he said the word engagement
a grin of all grins spread across his
exultant face.

Oliver could tell the Master had something
to tell and if he could extract it from him,
he was surely going to try.

After quite awhile of cajoling, Eriik
finally couldn't help but share the news
with Oliver, who was more than happy for
them both. He had always been treated well
in Eriik's household, certainly not like a
slave. It had happened slowly at first, as
he taught Eriik English and all things about
England. "Off to the market for the coming
dinner then," He was very anxious to meet
these priests and speak of religion and
other subjects he could not speak of here.

Lillian heard of the missionaries and was
eager to speak with them as well. She hoped
they were from somewhere near English soil
and could tell her news of her family and
friends. She had built a life here but
still missed her father and would love news
of him. She whiled away the morning
arranging for their visit, making sure the
great room looked its best and helping
Geirhild with her preparations.

Later on in the morning, Eriik showed up
with several priests and introduced them to
everyone, waiting until the last for
Lillian.

"And Lady Lillian, these are the priests
from the west, close to your home if I'm not
mistaken, my dear. They will dine with us
tonight as our honored guests."

"Wonderful news, my lord." She was very
excited but kept her eagerness in check.
She noticed one particular priest who kept
looking at her with what looked like
disdain. She must be imagining it. They
had never even met each other before. She

could have sworn she heard him quietly call
the people here heathens but couldn't have
sworn to it. What a way to win the hearts
of the local people. She thought he was
looking at her in a hateful manner. *Perhaps
he is judging me as Eriik's paramour. Judge
not lest ye be judged.* Well perhaps she
should be judged. But he wasn't going to be
the man to do it! He still made her very
uneasy. *Well he can go to bloody hell.
Oops, that wasn't very lady like,* she
thought, and she giggled.

She didn't have the time or patience to let
this priest, who she was probably imagining
everything about him anyway, ruin her day.
She would be able to talk to the others at
dinner about England and home, and she felt
better. Everything seemed well in hand, so
she retired to her chamber to rest,
realizing just how much she was looking
forward to this evening.

Eriik was also looking forward to this
evening, but for very different reasons!

While the main staff was working through the
day preparing for dinner along with many
guests, a few of the priests started feeling
a bit at home and quietly asked questions
about the Thorennson bastion and the
beautiful countryside surrounding it.
Amazing how much can be learned when the
right questions are asked by innocent men of
the cloth. Just the appropriate amount of
questions with lots of interesting
information of travels, foreign lands,
beautiful silks and spices to trade and the
stories to follow. Perhaps some ale, then

there is so much to tell and so much to
hear. And no one really noticed when one of
the priests sidled away from the group with
a sardonic grin on his face and a plan in
his pocket. *Now to the lady.*

Chapter 19

A maid knocked softly on Lillian's door.
"Yes, come in."

"Lady Lillian, there is a priest who says he
has word of your father in desperate times
and must talk with you."

Lillian sat up almost tumbling the chair
over, "Yes, yes, bring him to me, please, at
once!"

"Miss he will not see you in the manor. He
feels unsafe here with the Master. He will
only see you outside. He told me he has
found the tunnel under the manor and will
meet you there. He has your father's ring,
an emerald signet ring, and a letter meant
only for you."

Lillian started prattling in English and the
maid couldn't understand a word she was
saying so she just stood there dumbfounded.
"Oh I'm sorry, tell this man I'll meet him
in the tunnel in one half hour. He better
be there with the ring and the letter!

"Lady he insists you come alone or he'll
disappear and you won't see him again."

"Sidrid, did he speak to you himself in your
language?"

"No, he had a translator."

"Thank you dear. If you would, help me
dress and then run on and do whatever you
need to. I hate to way lay you but it looks

as if I need to get dressed now. And please
don't breathe a word of this to anyone."

"Yes my lady."

She put on the dress she was planning to
wear to dinner since she would have no time
to change with this clandestine meeting
taking place before dinner. She hoped
making her way through the labyrinth of the
dank and musty tunnel wouldn't completely
ruin the new frock she had picked out. Why
was this priest making it so difficult, why
couldn't he have just brought the ring and
Father's letter to her at dinner? He seems
to insist on making this covert. "Perhaps
other priests feel the same way about
Eriik," she thought. *Still no reason to
take me on a wild goose chase.* The farther
she went, the angrier she became. She
should have told Eriik and had him come with
her and straighten this whole thing out.
Knowing about this would have made him
furious! Just about the time she decided to
turn back, she heard a voice shouting her
name.

"Lady Lillian, it's me Ulric. I'm here,
just a little farther."

"Oh thank goodness, I was just about to turn
around."

"That would not have been a good idea." He
retorted, his eyes seemed to gaze furiously
at her.

She really wished now that Eriik was behind
her.

"Okay, you've gotten my full attention, so please let me see my father's letter.

"Of course princess."

He pulled it out of his robes, crumpled and soiled and handed it to Lillian, holding the torch so she could read it."

Sweet Pea,

I'm writing you in hopes this finds you well. I am bereft to tell you your mother has succumbed to the sickness that took many of our fine people and I am now alone. I miss you so very much. Lord Montfort has put a rescue mission in place and I am in his debt. I hope to see you soon.

Your loving father.

She looked at Ulric with amazement, "You're here to take me home?"

"Yes. We should leave immediately."

Her mind was racing. She could go home if she wanted to…but she didn't. She could not, would not leave Eriik. How obvious it was all of a sudden here in this dark, musty tunnel. She was already home.

She looked steadily at Ulric and said in no uncertain terms, "I'm sorry you made such a long and treacherous trip to take me home, however I am already home. I will be going nowhere with you except to the great room for dinner." She smiled a gracious smile. I can assure you, however, that nothing will happen to you at the manor."

"I'm fairly sure they would not approve of what I'm about to do."

"And what is that?" She was still smiling.

He brought his hand back and with all the force he could muster, slapped Lillian full in the face until her head snapped back and hit the rock of the wall hard.

She couldn't believe what had just happened. Was this a bad dream or had a man of the cloth just slapped her violently?

She was gasping and there was blood in her mouth. All she could say was, "Why?"

"Well *lady,*" he spat, "Mostly because I've been wanting to do that for a very long time. This just seemed like the right moment.

"But why would you do that? You came to rescue me. We just met, you couldn't possibly hate me enough to do such a thing."

"Oh nay princess, I have known you many years. You see, your highness, while you were parading around your grand castle like a bloody deity in the finest silks and velvets, feasting every eve, the peasants, like myself, were in the fields, laboring, barely keeping our bellies full. I decided long ago that an honest day's work gets a man sodding nowhere. That's especially true when regal scum like you and your father hold court. Now get going." He grabbed her roughly and started leading her out of the tunnel.

Lillian was still in shock. As she got her bearings, she broke loose and started to run back up the tunnel, but before she got too far, two other men who seemed to be lying in wait for her, grabbed her and brought her back.

"Lillian, now that we've gotten the most important introductions out of the way, I'll tell you my name is indeed Ulric, but I'm obviously not a priest, monk, man of the cloth or anything else even slightly akin to honest. My friends here aren't either. Ivar here has been traveling with priests for awhile but instead of spreading the lord's word, he's been spreading each of the countries' wealth straight into his pocket. They all laughed. It's been dreadful playing the good priests all the way here with those virtuous idiots. The other two shook their heads. We clear about this now?"

"No, I don't understand."

"What about my father's ring?"

"Yes indeed, here is his ring. He took his hand out of the robe and her father's signet ring was on the vile man's hand. She wanted to spit on him but decided that wouldn't be a smart thing to do.

"Oh, you're detestable. This makes no sense. You come all this way to rescue me and now you're kidnapping me?"

"I'm warning you, shut up or I'll hit you again!"

They walked on and on through the tunnel in silence and the more they walked the more Lillian expected Eriik to show up like he did when she was lost in the forest, but it was not to be. He probably didn't even know she was missing. That thought brought about serious dread.

Right before they exited the tunnel into the woods, Ulric gave Lillian a severe warning. "This is how it's going to work. We have a demanding trip ahead of us and you're not going to make it any easier. So, you better pull your own weight and not give us any trouble or you don't even want to know what I will do to you. The only reason you're not dead right now is because of the lord."

"The lord? My father?"

"No, Lord Montford."

Lillian froze. She couldn't speak or move. She was frozen in time. "Wait a minute. Lord Montfort isn't trying to save me, he's kidnapping me?"

"You're a bright girl. For some reason Lord Montfort wants you alive and well. He's the one who financed this little missionary trip in the first place. You think he gives a damn about bringing God to these heathens? I'll tell you I sure as hell don't. The god we pray to is money and our god has been very generous or we wouldn't have come to this desolate land. Now we can leave religion to the priests and get you back to Lord Montfort so we can collect the remainder of our gold."

"And how do you propose we get back to England?" Lillian looked defiant.

"We will return as we came, thru Denmark, the Frankish Empire, Kent, Essex, Marcia, and finally to England. It's a hard journey, but money makes everything possible, so shut up and behave yourself or you'll be sorry."

"Oh really."

"Don't tempt me to slap you again because it would be my pleasure so long as I don't ruin that pretty face of yours. That's really all the lord cares about, and believe me when I tell you a bruise or two will heal by the time we arrive."

"Let me warn you, when Eriik finds out what you've done, whatever becomes of me, the three of you will be wishing you had never come close to these lands. You would not believe what these men can do to other men, especially if you're their enemy. And trust me, you will become their enemy!"

The looks on their faces became a little less arrogant.

Surely Eriik would notice she was missing and come looking for her. She would only have to wait a matter of minutes and he would ride up on Kriger and sweep her up in his arms outside the tunnel. Why had she been so stupid? She wanted nothing more right at this moment than to be in his strong arms. How much time she had wasted trying to deny her feelings for him.

Just as they exited the tunnel, Ulric tossed a piece of linen at her and demanded that she write a good bye note to Eriik.

"And make it good, or the last thing we'll do is lop off your lovers head and return it to Lord Montfort. He would enjoy that."

"What am I supposed to say?"

"You'll think of something convincing."

She started to write in English when Ulric grabbed it away from her and raised his hand, "I should slap you til your neck snaps. Don't try me girl. I am not that stupid. Write in his language, and don't think none of us can read it, so don't try anything else or I will carry out my threat and it will be for all of our amusement."

She wrote with the Norse words and symbols and even though Lillian had made great strides in that area, the fading light and the insistence that she hurry gave her little time to try to sort out what to do. She had to think! As she paused, Ulric, in no uncertain terms gave the order for one of the men to remain and not return without Eriik's head.

"You will die trying." Lillian said with assurance she didn't feel.

"Are you so sure of that, lady, that you are willing to take the chance that his head won't come back in a bag? It would be so easy to catch him off his guard. He would never suspect a priest, after all." Ulric grinned sarcastically.

Lillian did her best to swallow down the nausea that notion caused, "Why do you think I even care? He kidnapped me after all."

"Let's just say I have a hunch." He looked at her as if she was some immoral creature. "We've paid attention while we've been here and it certainly hasn't been difficult to figure out. Now write before I forget my orders and carve you up like an evening's feast."

She started to scream, but felt a dirty, smelly handkerchief being stuffed in her mouth. She began to gag and was afraid she might throw up.

Lillian continued to write, hoping she had said what was needed, but not obvious enough that Ulric's man would notice. Ulric nodded to one of the men and as he read slowly and laboriously, he nodded back, "Seems alright to me. She says she's leaving this god forsaken country to be with her lovely or loving mother and father, something like that. Nothing about us or leaving against her will. Ulric concurred, they started off quickly, and she was roughly dragged through the countryside to a heavily wooded area where another man was waiting impatiently with some fine horses for all of them, and several others to spare. Superb horses such as these must have cost quite a few coins. She wanted to know if the revolting Lord Montfort had fingers that reached this far to finance all this but nothing audible could be heard with the filthy rag fouling her mouth.

Lillian was hoping with all her might to
wake up to find this had all been a horrible
nightmare and Eriik was sleeping peacefully
by her side, but it was not to be. It was
all very real and seemed as if it was only
going to get worse.

Chapter 20

The dinner preparations were going as planned. Eriik came home in a jaunty mood, arriving from some very boring meetings with his advisors where he could hardly keep his mind on the subjects at hand. He could only think of Lillian and those silken thighs and long sable hair spread across the bed, her emerald green eyes looking at him, waiting for him to make love to her. Many times throughout the day, Bjorn had to shout at him to make him aware of where he was and what they were doing there. Finally the tedious day was over and he couldn't wait to get home where his lovely Lillian waited.

He entered his chambers expecting to find her, hoping she might be in a state of undress, but disappointed to discover an empty room. He recognized just how empty the room really was without her. With all the English priests in town he was sure she had lost track of time hearing the stories from her home. He was glad she was able to do so, but yearned for her to want to stay with him. He had already decided to ask her to join with him officially, legally, but offer to take her back to England if that was what she wished. That thought brought him actual physical pain and his breath came in small gasps as he contemplated life without her. He would dress and await her return downstairs at dinner. He wanted her to be able to enjoy these priests' visit and

give her no grief about it. He only wanted
to give her love. Oh, if only she could
return that love in kind. He had prayed to
the gods that she could and would be able to
do so.

He finished dressing with one special
addition, his grandmother's ring tucked
inside his tunic, anticipating seeing it
soon on Lillian's delicate finger. He
thought his grandmother would be pleased.
He wished some of his relatives were still
alive to see him wed, but Bjorn was like a
brother to him in every way and he couldn't
imagine a brother of blood being any closer.

He went downstairs smiling and declaring
good eve to all in a booming voice.
Everyone in the household could tell the
master was in good spirits this twilight.

Eriik had invited many guests for dinner
that night in anticipation, actually hope,
of a celebration. As the food started to
appear, as well as the guests, Eriik started
to feel a strange apprehension that he shook
off as ridiculous, but the feeling hung on.
He ignored it, thinking he was just nervous,
after all he was getting ready to change his
life forever. He didn't think he felt
anxious, but that must be it. When the
priests arrived but Lillian did not, the
apprehension immediately turned into
something more. He asked the leader of the
group, Ambrose, as calmly as he could
manage, "Where is Lady Lillian? Is she on
her way?"

Ambrose looked confused, "I'm sorry, my lord, I haven't seen her all day."

Eriik's uneasiness became absolute terror. In a roar, he asked the entire household, "Has anyone seen Lady Lillian?"

One of the chamber maids timidly raised her hand, looking terrified.

Seeing her fear, Eriik tried to appear less frightening, "Please tell me lass."

"Master, one of the English priests came to me to get Lady Lillian to meet him in the tunnel."

He couldn't stop the dread in his voice, "And."

"The priest said he had news of Lady Lillian's father. He had her father's signet ring and a letter. He would not meet her here because of his fear of…"

"Of…"

"You." She couldn't look Eriik in the eye.

"By the gods, I will kill him." His fists were clenched and his face was bright red. "To the tunnel."

Eriik and all of his men ran to the tunnel and through it with torches looking for anything out of the ordinary. Eriik knew this tunnel well. He and Bjorn had played there as children. It seems there were signs of a struggle and it constricted Eriik's throat with alarm, but at the exit to the tunnel, they found a piece of linen staked to a tree with writing on it. Eriik couldn't bear to look, so Bjorn started to read it to himself.

I have finally found a way out and I'm taking it gladly. I am going home to my loving mother and father, leaving this god forsaken place to be free at last, to be with the husband my mother chose for me. I want nothing more to do with you, Eriik, and your heathen friends. You should not follow me.

Lilian.

It was no easy task, as it was written in a scrawl, but what was written there would surely tear his friend to shreds, perhaps not physically, but worse. Bjorn started reading it aloud but Eriik stopped him after Lillian said she had found a way out and was taking it gladly. He couldn't stand anymore. He didn't see the point, she was gone and he was alone.

Bjorn handed the letter to Eriik but he couldn't look at it. All the color had completely drained from his face. He was a broken man. He had given his heart to Lillian and she had torn it to shreds. He didn't think he would ever get over this. No, damn her to hell! Obviously she had been pretending the whole time. He was so sure she cared for him. What an idiot. She played him well. Just enough time and freedom to find a way out. Well, he could have any woman he wanted and that's what he intended to do, dammit, what he *would* do. *But why did he want only this woman?* By the

gods he would never taste those words cross
his lips!

As Eriik was turning around sadly for home,
Lillian was riding swiftly away…from home.

Chapter 21

As Lillian's nightmare continued and the
journey dragged on, she had given up on
seeing Eriik ride up on his magnificent war
horse to save her so she could tell him how
she really felt. She loved him. She wanted
to spend the rest of her life with him and
bear his children. It was as simple as
that. Obviously he had not recognized the
inconsistencies of the letter meant for him,
to realize she had been taken against her
will. She had written in a messy scrawl as
a clue, but perhaps that was one of the
reasons he hadn't picked up on it, he
probably couldn't even read most of it. Oh,
what an idiot she was. Eriik had never even
seen her lessons. He would not have known
whether she could write his language well or
not. If only she had had a little more time
to think. There was no use going over what
she should have done, they were far away
from Eriik now and getting closer to the
foul Lord Montfort each day. Her only hope
was her father. Perhaps he had changed his
mind and would save her from her fate.

★★★★

One evening, as Lillian lay on her bedroll
staring at the stars, she felt more than saw
someone standing over her. She felt a hand
suddenly clasp over her mouth, and a soft
whisper in her ear, "If I take my hand away
and you scream, I'll slit your throat right
here and now, do you understand?"

Lillian nodded. It was the man called
Rowan.

She said in a low, quiet voice, "What do you
want?

"Well, I'm feeling rather lonely tonight and
decided I would pay you a long overdue
visit. I thought it was high time you knew
what it was like to be with a real man, not
some pagan, and that time is now wench."

He started to caress her cheek but she
turned in disgust, "I demand you get away
from me immediately."

"Oh you demand, do you, miss holier than
thou?"

"Don't you think your reward will be
compromised if you continue this rape or
worse, slit my throat?"

"Now, now my little harlot, I certainly
wouldn't call this rape, it's just the two
of us getting to know each other a little
better and I don't think I'll have to get
violent, it's not like you've never seen one
of these before, is it my sweet?" He pulled
his pants down so Lillian could see his
swollen flesh.

She thought she may retch, "By God, I would
rather throw myself into the sea than feel
your filthy hands touch my flesh."

His face suddenly turned and she saw the
rage in his eyes and hand ball into a fist,
coming straight for her face. She readied
herself for the blow but it never came. She

heard a loud crack and as she allowed herself to open her eyes she saw that Ulric had knocked Rowan to the ground with a malicious punch to his head.

"Don't be thanking me too soon your highness, I wouldn't mind a minute or two between your tender thighs myself. Believe me, I would love to ram myself into you so hard your teeth would chatter, just to humble you if nothing more. I don't understand why it would matter to Lord Montfort, you're already soiled goods anyway, but for some reason, it does," he finished with a scornful look in his eyes.

"I simply can't allow my reward to be challenged because of weakness of the flesh, including my own." He sounded disappointed. "We'll be seeing the good lord soon so best prepare yourself. He'll be quite glad to have you in his grasp once again," he grinned a self-satisfied grin and walked away dragging the unconscious Rowan with him.

The thought of seeing the despicable Lord Montfort again made Lillian's stomach turn. Perhaps she could run away, but they always kept to the back roads and Ulric had her well-guarded at all times, making that almost impossible. Trying to run off in the middle of nowhere could easily lead to an early demise, so she kept her hopes on her father to see what an evil man Lord Montfort was and save her when they arrived, which according to Ulric was very soon now. Trying to get any sleep with that horrid fate looming close was unattainable. She

spent most of her time thinking of Eriik and
wondering if he had forgotten about her and
gone on to more fertile fields by now. That
thought brought about a hopelessness that
she simply couldn't abide. She must have
fallen asleep because when she opened her
eyes, it was morning and she remembered
seeing the most handsome face with the
bluest eyes, golden hair, and thick corded
muscles arriving to save her. Oh for it to
have been more than a dream, for him to
materialize now that the sun was up and her
eyes were open. She would love to feel
those broad, hard muscles close around her,
protecting her from the ugliness of the
world like a cocoon. Tears came unbidden to
her eyes, but she held them back as Ulric
came into view. She would not have him see
her cry. She straightened her spine, looked
at him defiantly, mounted, and they rode on
toward her frightening future.

Chapter 22

This day had been a particularly difficult
day. They seemed to stop for nothing,
eating jerky while in the saddle. Lillian
was almost falling asleep while plodding
along when she heard the nervous chatter
amongst the men and tried to focus on what
the excitement was all about. When she saw
the monstrous castle rising out of the
colorful streaks of the last of the sun's
rays, a lump formed in her throat she could
not swallow. She had never seen that
citadel before, but she didn't have to, she
knew who resided there. She pulled her
horse up short, but Ulric was right behind
her to spur her mount to continue on. She
was almost to the point she had been
dreading now since her mother had sold her
out for greed. How could her entire life
have been turned upside down in just a few
short months? More importantly, how could
she have found love in the most impossible
place imaginable and now lost it, being
replaced by the most foul man she had ever
met? As they pushed closer, she prayed to
God to please somehow save her, but if for
some reason this was his will, let her meet
it with dignity. Ulric grabbed Lillian's
reins and brought her mount to a canter as
they closed the gap to the fortress, and as
they pulled the horses to a stop at the
front gate, Lord Montfort himself came out
to greet them, along with his staff.

A smiling man stepped forward and said
happily, "Ah Lady Lillian, we haven't had

the pleasure, my name is James Montfort. I'm Simon's cousin. I'm so pleased to make your acquaintance."

He was so pleasant, Lillian was almost happy to meet him, "Nice to meet you too, my lord."

Then Simon Montfort stepped forward with a leering grin across his ugly face.

"Yes, welcome Lady Lillian. It's been far too long since I've enjoyed your company. Don't mind my half-witted cousin, I'm sure you're exhausted so I'll accept your thanks later at dinner. I'm sure you don't quite have the words at this time to thank me for your rescue from the villainess pagans that assaulted your home and took you hostage. I, however, can think of many ways for you to repay me," he said under his breath. He had a wicked smile glued to his face. James, on the other hand, had lost his smile completely.

Lillian didn't say the words that immediately came to mind. She knew if she reacted as she wished, there would be hell to pay, so she asked demurely, "Yes, I'm quite weary from the journey. Might I freshen up, please?"

"Of course, my dear. I have a chamber ready for you." He nodded and a maid motioned Lillian to follow her. Nothing would feel better at the moment than to be away from all these dreadful men and be alone. She told the maid she would be fine on her own and as soon as the chamber door closed, she sighed with relief. Now, if she could just

fly out the window like a bird, everything
would be fine. She took a minute to look
around the room and was horrified to find
everything she could ever want neatly
arranged, from brushes and mirrors, to
frocks that looked just her size. This was
like a nightmare but she knew she would not
be waking up any time soon. Once again, she
was asking herself if she should throw
herself from the window, but this time she
really meant it. She could see so clearly
now what had really gone on inside her head
when she was with Eriik and how her
stubbornness had kept them apart so long. If
she only had that time back, how she would
change it all.

She went to the door and just as she
expected, it was locked. The locked door
brought back so many memories, good ones
now. She couldn't help the onslaught of
tears that overwhelmed her as she wept for
all the time wasted and all the love lost.

Chapter 23

Lillian forced herself to change into the
nightclothes provided by the lord, even
though putting them on made her shiver. She
simply had to rid herself of the clothes she
had had on for so many endless weeks,
washing only parts of them in streams they
found along the way. She wouldn't admit
even to herself how wonderful the silk felt
against her skin. If only it had been from
someone, anyone else. She wouldn't think of
it anymore. At least she was warm and dry
and had clean clothes. She spied the brush
and was in heaven again as she got to brush
the awful tangles out of her hair and lie
down on a soft bed. If only the lock on the
door was locked from her side. The weeks on
the trail and now lying on the comfortable
bed in the silken nightgown must have been
the impetus to cause her to be slumbering
peacefully in no time, no nightmares marring
her sleep this night and no lord making an
appearance.

She awoke the next morning refreshed and
ready to meet the day. She had decided just
before drifting off that Lord Montfort
didn't know it yet, but he had met his
match. She was not willing to go to his
marriage bed without a fight. She would be
no lamb to the slaughter. She still had her
father and if history was any lesson, he
could be persuaded. Her mother was gone now
and while she tried to be saddened by that
fact, respect that she was her mother was
all she could summon. However with her

mother's greed for political gain gone now, perhaps she could sway her father. A little common sense should prevail. Frederick was always a very practical man. Her mind made up, she would be the genteel lady she was brought up to be and look forward to seeing her father. These social weddings usually took months to plan so perhaps she had the time she needed. She picked out a particularly fetching frock and readied herself for when she would be allowed outside the bedroom door. This was another conversation they would need to have soon. The future Lady Montfort should not be locked up like a common prisoner. Where would she go after all? The only place would be her father's home and that was entirely too far to go without an escort, which was exactly what she intended to request soon. Until then she would play her role to the best of her ability. The disgusting Lord Montfort didn't know who he was up against.

Speaking of the lock, she heard the bolt tumble and the door opened abruptly as the lord regally entered the room with nothing on but a well adorned wrapper. "I've been thinking, dear, there is no need for me to wait for the marriage bed, you have, after all, been quite the trollop. You are already soiled, my dove, you are certainly no virgin. I've been assured of this by my men on good authority. They listened to the talk of the townspeople and the whispers of the servants of the pagan Jarl to know exactly how you felt and what you were doing with the heathen devil." He walked toward her and opened the wrapper as if he were

unwrapping a special Christmas package. He
stood there before her naked, with his bones
showing through his white, pasty skin and
his sex member flopping unresponsive between
his legs. His lank stringy hair hung
lifeless on his scrawny neck. Looking at
this poor excuse of a man brought to memory
Eriik's beautiful golden hair falling
gloriously about his strong, thick neckline,
where his pulse beat fiercely and the saber
of his maleness hard and thick, reaching for
his belly. She blushed thinking of such
things and smiled in spite of herself. She
could almost see his strong, muscular frame
standing tall and formidable in front of
her. Looking now at Montfort was a
disgusting sight to behold and chills went
up Lillian's spine, but she made certain to
conceal it. She had seen two men in her
entire lifetime naked and the comparison was
woeful. She was standing there with her
mouth hanging open and decided a saucy reply
was in order. "You're men don't think I'm a
blushing bride do they now? Well let me
tell you something, lord," she spat the word
out like venom.

"It's one thing to be raped by rampaging
Vikings who laid siege to my home and took
me hostage, and entirely another matter to
be raped by the great Lord Montfort, held in
such high regard by the lords and ladies of
the land. What do you think will happen to
your precious reputation when they find out,
and they will find out, unless, of course,
you plan to murder me. Is that your plan,
my lord?

Montfort seemed to turn an even whiter shade of pale and sputtered, "Of course not, we will be wed. You will be Lady Montfort!"

"I see. Then there will be no sexual folly outside of wedlock, and that's the last I will hear of it, or see of it."

Lillian didn't think she would ever be able to get that vision of him naked out of her head. She couldn't even contemplate the vision becoming a nightly routine.

She whirled around as to signal the end of that particular conversation and silently asked Eriik's forgiveness for even mentioning the word rape when speaking of him. He never once treated her with anything but kindness, even when tethering her to him. Everything she remembered now, even that, was remembered with fondness.

Lord Montfort sped out of the room. He was enraged, and on his way to his own chamber he grabbed a chamber maid, dragging her with him by her hair. The maid, Theona, knew better than to scream. He slammed the door and threw her down to the floor. He sat in his favorite chair and crooked his finger to have her crawl to him as if she were a dog. He opened his wrapper and it was very clear what he expected her to do. It wasn't the first time. He pushed her head into his crotch until she thought she might suffocate. His sorry excuse of a cock was so limp and soft, Theona had a difficult time getting it into her mouth and as she was trying, he brought her head up, "Having a *hard* time dearie?" He slapped her so hard it actually hurt his hand. That made him feel a little better, especially picturing Lillian in her place. He tore the bodice of her dress and looked at her naked from the waist up. It did nothing to arouse him. He slapped her again and he felt some movement between his legs. Pushing her face down again between his legs, he grabbed his ridding crop and flogged her again and again until he could see red welts standing out on her bare back. He took his fingernails and pricked the welts until they bled, leaving fine trails of blood streaking down her fair skin and that's when he really started to feel stimulated. Her face was starting to turn black and blue and her back was streaked with blood and that's when he was finally firm enough for her to be able to put her mouth around him, saying not a word, crying not a tear. It took forever, but she continued until it was finished. Montfort called for his man servant to take Theona to a room to be tended to until she was fit to work again. "See now my dear, you'll be able to lie around in bed, avoiding work for a few days. Aren't you the lucky wench."

Chapter 24

The next morning, as Lillian heard the bolt
slip off the door once again, she regally
strutted through it as any Lady of the Realm
might do. She looked as if any dissent
would not be tolerated. She gingerly
touched each stair as if she were floating
on air, and it seemed the entire castle came
to a stop to see the vision descend the
great staircase. Even Lord Montfort came to
a halt and stared.

She waited to be seated by the lord at the
head of the table to be served as the lady
she was, and all kinds of activity flared as
well. The lady is ready to break her fast
and the staff buzzed. Lillian wanted Lord
Montfort to think that he wasn't going to
have as much trouble with her as he had once
feared. She was sure he had a plan if
things went awry, so she needed to convince
him that perhaps she had been mistreated in
the Norse land and was ready for English
genteel living again, reserved only for the
upper crust. She needed him to believe it
absolutely, at least for the time being.
Maybe he would think she had been taught a
lesson by the horrible Norsemen. She needed
the time.

"My dear lord, when may I see my father?
It's been much too long since I laid eyes on
his dear face and since my poor mother's
passing, well…" She dabbed a tear from her
eye with her handkerchief and made it seem
as if she were quite distraught.

Montfort thought for a moment, "I was thinking we would have an engagement party as soon as the invitations can be sent out by courier and your father, my dear friend, could visit us for awhile, and you and he can grieve together, then hopefully be able to put it behind you to plan the happy occasion of our wedding. Why, it will be the social gathering of the season."

"Oh I have no doubt of that my lord."

Lord Montfort smiled a self-satisfied smile and Lillian could tell that she had, at least for the most part, put his mind somewhat at ease. The troll actually thought she was looking forward to marrying him. If she could just keep from retching at the mere idea, it would probably help immensely. There was a plan forming and she had some thinking and scheming to do. In the meantime she couldn't slip from the snobbish, spoiled, English aristocratic lady she needed to be, the kind she could never abide. She would play it like a game. So, let the games begin.

She had to hope that her father would agree to save her from this god forsaken fate when she got the chance to talk to him in private. Until that time, she would play Lady Montfort in waiting with flare. This would be the only way to hold the snake at bay until she could secure a way out of the viper's nest.

Chapter 25

The hours became days and the days melted
into weeks. Eriik felt empty, trying to
fill them fighting too hard and drinking too
much. Many of the comely girls in the
village tried to assuage his grief,
especially Helgi, Lady Asgaut, a very
beautiful girl who was quite smitten with
him. She was determined to make him forget
the Saxon whore, as she called her. Helgi
started showing up on Eriik's arm more often
than not. Eriik knew she wanted some sort
of commitment and would be sorely
disappointed when it didn't come forth. He
knew she felt they were having quite the
romance and the only bastion she hadn't
conquered yet was his bed, not that she
hadn't tried. Eriik was furious with
Lillian for ruining that part of his life.
He used to be ready for any comely maid just
by thinking of taking her to bed. But now,
when he thought of loving, all he could
think of was beautiful dark hair and
smoldering, and apparently lying eyes. He
would get over this in time, by the gods he
would, however he would never give his heart
to a woman again. They would be able to
gain access to only one part of his body and
it would sure as hell not be his heart.

One night after dinner Helgi seemed
especially determined to get into Eriik's
robes, as she started a slow, sensual dance
for him, leisurely, erotically, caressing
her body, and swaying her hips, inviting him
none too subtly. It was meant to inflame,

and it succeeded. She licked her full, sensuous lips, gliding to Eriik as if on air. She ran her fingers through his long, thick hair and kissed him, trying to run her tongue across his lips. It should have excited him but for some reason, he backed up just the slightest bit. This did nothing to discourage Helgi. She sidled up to him again and took his hand to lead him upstairs. As she started for his bed chamber, he led her away to another room. It was nicely appointed but nothing like his private chamber. Helgi had found out from the maids early in their relationship which room was his and could barely hide her disappointment when he turned to another. She closed the door and piece by piece began to disrobe. When she was standing there before Eriik in nothing but a very revealing chemise, she reached for his hand, but he held back. He couldn't understand what he was waiting for and neither could she. She was picturesque, standing there almost naked with her long blonde hair spilling about her shoulders, but all he could see was dark hair cascading down a slender back with emerald eyes looking at him with…longing? He thought at the time that it may have even been love.

She slowly removed her chemise from one shoulder, then the other, at the same time opening his shirt. She chafed his chest with her full breasts and her nipples hardened as Eriik watched. She started untying his breeches, but he stopped her. As she continued her sexual assault on him and he did nothing but stop her at every turn, she became frustrated, but still

unwavering. She backed up and lay on the
bed, rolling the hard pink buds of her
nipples in between her fingertips. She
slowly opened her thighs and tantalizingly
stroked herself until it was evident she was
wet and ready for his advance. Eriik was
hard, so hard and heavy, swollen with lust,
but still seemingly trapped in one place,
staring at this lovely woman but thinking
only of Lillian. He realized that even
though his body could deliver whatever he
asked of it, his mind was not ready. He
walked over to Helgi and gently pulled the
robes on the bed over her shoulders,
shielding her breasts from his view.

"Helgi, you are a beautiful sight and any
man would be lucky to have you but I'm
afraid I'm not that man right now, as my
heart is broken and it would not do you
justice to take you when I'm thinking of no
one but the lass who did the breaking."

"Your heart is broken," she said
sarcastically. If you would just give me
the chance you would forget the Saxon harlot
as you should not have given her your heart
in the first place."

"Perhaps, but I do not want to be with any
other woman than Lillian right now and I'm
not going to force myself to bed a woman
just to prove I can. I know I can
physically but I want more, so much more. I
don't understand it but the gods work in
their own way and I know enough to listen.
I will not be doing anything to you tonight
that I will be regretting later. Helgi, I'm
sorry. Please get dressed and leave. As

I've tried to explain, it's not you, sweetheart, it's me."

"Eriik Thorennson, you are being an ass and you will regret this one day." She was yelling at him as he turned and quickly left the room with Helgi alone, gasping for breath, embarrassed, and angry.

He saddled Kriger and galloped out to the crossroads where he found Molly that night Lillian went missing. The night he first realized just how much she meant to him. Tears streamed down his face. The first time in his entire life he had allowed himself to cry. Not for his father, not for friends when they entered Valhalla on the battlefield…never. But this woman brought him to tears. He walked, stared at the stars, prayed to the gods and thought hard about his and Lillian's time together. Since she had been gone, he had been in a rage, telling himself that she was simply lying the whole time she had supposedly come to him willingly, seemingly caring, even with love in her eyes. That had been his hope at least. Something in the back of his mind kept bothering him, kept pestering him. He simply couldn't keep convincing himself that it was all a lie. After what seemed like hours, he returned and drank a few pints in the great room. He decided to do something he hadn't had enough courage to do since Lillian left. He retrieved the note and started to read it. He read it over and over and couldn't stop the ringing in his ears that something was definitely not right. He bellowed throughout the household, "Oliver!"

After several bellows, Oliver appeared rather disheveled and tousled but heeded Eriik's call willingly.

"Oliver, take a look at this letter and tell me what you think."

He looked at the letter, "Oh Lord Thorennson, I would hate to impose on something so personal."

"Nonsense, I feel something is not right and I want you to read it carefully."

Oliver took the letter and read it word for word under the candlelight. He read it meticulously. His expression went from dejected and saddened for his lord to anger in a matter of moments.

"What is it?" Eriik demanded.

"You are right my lord, something is truly wrong about this letter. In fact, many things. Firstly, Lady Lillian misspelled her own name. Most importantly though, this letter is written in a scrawl whereas Lady Lillian wrote in a neat and precise manner."

Eriik was looking on pensively.

Oliver continued, "She speaks of Lord Montfort in a loving way as if he was a good man when she thought he was vile and evil. She spoke of him so many times as such. And her mother, as loving, when Lady Lillian felt she was greedy and indifferent. Forgive me my lord."

"Nonsense, I want your honesty. What do you make of it?"

"I think she wrote this under duress, not of her own volition at all. I swear my lord, with everything that is holy to me, I am sure of it."

"Oh by the gods! Eriik struck the table with such force that the goblet crashed to the floor, spilling the contents. She was taken right from under my nose and I did nothing to stop it? And to make matters worse, I've let weeks go by without raising a hand to get her back! What kind of man am I?"

"Lord, you did not know. The pain and heartbreak was too much to bear."

"No, I condemned her without a word or a chance for her to tell me herself. I never even gave a thought to the possibility that she might have been taken against her will even though we saw sure signs of a struggle in the tunnel when we followed her. I will never forgive myself for this, especially if anything, I mean anything has happened to her. If one hair on her head has been damaged, I will slay myself willingly."

"Never say that my lord."

"Oliver, wake up the household." As he looked around, he noticed almost everyone was already up. "Well anyone who isn't up already," he said sheepishly. "Take as many as needed to notify my men. We must start to prepare for a sea voyage to England. We are going a raiding, but not for gold this time!"

****

Eriik thought he would go out of his mind by the time it took the men to get ready to sail. Bjorn was his steady right hand, as usual, but everything was moving at a snail's pace.

"Eriik, we can't go up against the gods unprepared. It would be a fool's errand. Loki can be a trickster and he would doom us from the start if we don't prepare ourselves well."

"I know. I just can't believe I let hoodlums take Lillian right out of my own house. I'm supposed to be a great warrior and I can't keep one little girl safe."

"Admonish yourself all you like but it was not your fault."

"Then whose fault was it, yours?"

"Talking to you is impossible. We will be ready soon and out on the sea. You'll feel better there. One thing I don't understand though is how you know she's in England. She could be anywhere."

"Those priests, well not priests obviously, but whoever they really were, were indeed English and I can swear on my mother's soul they didn't just decide on a whim to take Lillian. I know who's behind this."

"You know them?"

"I know who sent them. Montfort! And I hope his god is looking the other way when I find him."

"And we'll be right behind you."

"Aye."

All was finally prepared and the longships glided out, coupling with the sea as long lost lovers coming together. Eriik took his turn at the rowing station. He had to expend some of his energy or he would tear someone to pieces and that someone was a long distance away. It felt good to have the oars pull against his muscles until they hurt and the cold salt water splash against his face. He could let go and for the first time in weeks, he felt like himself again. But this time he was angry and more than ready to feel bones crushing beneath his bare hands. It couldn't be soon enough for Eriik. He had always been the peaceful one, but that Eriik had disappeared for this voyage and a very different, vengeful Eriik had come along. He longed to have Lillian cradled in his arms and feel her lips on his. To feel her again, he would have crushed entire armies without a second thought. What if she *had* gone willingly and this was a fool's errand? He banished that thought from his mind. He would rather think of Montfort's body breaking in between his hands and that smirk being wiped off his ugly face for eternity. Yes, these thoughts made Eriik smile for the first time in weeks. He knew the gods were with them as the sun came out each and every day as well as a prevailing wind. The god Loki, the sky traveller, was not being the trickster, he must be blessing this journey after all. He could almost see Thor, hammer held high, smiling down upon them.

"Good tide my brothers."

Catherine Sharp
Viking's Desire146

"Good tide, Eriik."

Chapter 26

Lillian was so excited, she could hardly
stand still for the maid to help her dress.
Her father should be arriving today and
hopefully she wouldn't be in this beast's
lair too much longer. She still had not
been able to figure out how in the world she
would be able to get a message to Eriik to
tell him how she felt. She could not, would
not live the rest of her life without him.
She fervently hoped he had not gone on with
his life without her and it was already too
late. One step at a time. She had to get
out of this mess first.

As usual, she descended the steps with
grandeur and held her hand out to Lord
Montfort as a great lady to her gentleman.
It was always so hard for her to smile as
his cold, damp hand clamped over hers, but
she did so with aplomb.

"My lord, I've been meaning to ask you about
your friend Ulric." "Yes, my dear," he
replied politely as if they were already a
married couple.

"He is in possession of my father's signet
ring, and I would very much like to have it
back. Would you be so kind?"

"Of course. Your father gave it to me only
to convince you of our sincerity when
rescuing you."

"Very smart my lord. Even though I was
being held prisoner, I wouldn't have run off

with just anyone," she smiled a sweet, provocative smile.

She would rather have told him what he could do with his sincerity and what she would like to do to Ulric, but decided that would be lunacy at this time.

"I'll have it for you by the party."

"Thank you, my lord."

She was jumpy all day, waiting for her father. It felt as if she was waiting for judgment day. It actually was in a way. She couldn't imagine her father condemning her to a life with this monster. She knew he had done so before but that was with her mother's persuasiveness. Now it was her turn.

When she heard of her father's arrival, she couldn't simply wait, she ran outside and as her father opened the carriage door, she ran into his arms and for the first time since Ulric slapped her in the face, she felt safe and secure. Unfortunately too soon, she felt an unwelcome presence as Lord Montfort wiggled his way in between them, shaking her father's hand and placing his arm around her waist possessively. Her father's beaming face gave away his satisfaction with the present situation and Lillian's heart sank. *He doesn't know how I feel about the lord or Eriik. He thinks Lord Montfort bravely rescued me. I'll convince him otherwise, I have to!*

The day was spent pleasantly enough but she could never get rid of Montfort long enough to get a private word with her father. Finally she decided something radical must be done. As her father and Montfort were talking, she suddenly burst into tears. Both men looked concerned and her father ran to her, "Lillian, sweet pea, what in the world?"

"Oh father, it's just that we haven't talked about dear mother…"

"Yes, I guess I've been trying to avoid…" His eyes filled with tears.

Montfort looked exceedingly uncomfortable and excused himself so they could speak privately about their loss.

As soon as he left the room and closed the door, Lillian wiped her eyes and exploded with rage at having been literally kidnapped by Montfort's thugs, going on to explain everything that had happened since she first met Ulric in the tunnel from being slapped to the embarrassing evening of Montfort's appearance in her chamber naked. She pleaded with her father to save her, to take her home. She then explained that she was in love with Eriik, that he had shown her nothing but kindness and love in return. She didn't know how she could be with him again, but that was her desire. Lillian reminded him of his promise to her long ago, a marriage of love, not convenience or politics. Frederick was appalled at what had happened to her because of Lord Montfort and agreed to take her home immediately. He believed all along that she had been rescued from a horrible fate and that Montfort was a

hero. He certainly would never leave her to
marry someone she despised, especially since
that someone had kidnapped her with villains
who had mistreated her and brought her here
against her will. They would leave at first
light and he would help her find Eriik again
somehow. Lillian was ecstatic and was
hopeful for the first time since her first
meeting with Ulric in the tunnel below
Eriik's home.

"Father, don't say a word and don't let on.
We'll just get up early tomorrow and leave.
No one can be the wiser."

Lillian could barely sleep that night as
every nerve in her body was on edge, waiting
for the sun to wake the world, knowing she
would be gone and on her way home. Her
father had come through and saved her, just
as she had hoped. She was going to be free.
After they left this place, she would start
planning how to reach Eriik. Now she just
had to get through this endless night.

Just before the sun peaked over the horizon,
Lillian was dressed and ready to go. She
sneaked ever so quietly down the staircase
and went to the stable as she and her father
had planned. He should have already been
there with his driver, hitching up the
horses. Surely he wouldn't be late on this
very important day. She waited and waited
and was starting to really be concerned when
she heard him calling her name. The relief
was overwhelming. As she turned and ran to
the door, the sight she beheld was more
frightening than anything she had gone
through the past several months. Her father

was there, but so was Lord Montfort, and a man with a knife to her father's throat. Montfort had the most sadistic smile on his face. Her father looked truly scared.

"Just as I thought, trying to run away. Not the blushing bride after all."

"What in God's name do you think you're doing? Tell him to put that knife away. You can't be serious about hurting my father."

"Oh I'm dead serious. Put him under the staircase in chains. If he gives you any trouble, slit his throat."

Lillian started to cry.

"Real tears this time, my dear?"

"You damn horses ass, you bastard!"

"I'm afraid names will get you nowhere, now get your pretty ass in the house before I decide to do away with both of you."

He caressed her cheek with his unusually long fingernails and nodded to one of the other men who grabbed her none too gently and started back toward the main house, "Take her to my chamber."

Lillian was practically thrown on the bed and the door was bolted. She started to weep uncontrollably but stopped abruptly and dried her eyes. This would get her nowhere. She had to be ready when Montfort got there. She looked around for a weapon, anything. There were some liquor decanters. She could hit him over the head, but that would just

bring about his wrath when he came to and he
might do more than just terrorize her
father. The decanters made her think about
getting drunk in Eriik's chamber. If only
Eriik were here. She would love to see
Montfort in Eriik's solid, capable hands.
She couldn't think of one single thing she
could do, so she waited in abject fear. She
had no control over the situation and he
would do what he wanted. She didn't have to
wait long. The door opened and he had the
most hateful look on his face, she panicked.
Had he killed her father? Surely not, "Is
my father alright?"

"If alright means sitting in a damp, dark
cellar in chains, a guard with orders to
kill for any misdeed alright, then yes, of
course." He grinned.

"Tell me what you want, then let my father
go."

"You know what I want, what I will get, but
I don't think I will let your father go
anytime soon. He has to walk the bride down
the aisle after all, yes?"

"You are insane."

"Now, now. You are speaking of your
intended. However, now, since you've been
such a bitch, we don't have much time to
prepare for the wedding. We can't drag this
out since I have to keep my eyes, not to
mention a guard on you every minute of the
day. If you have any ideas of escaping,
please know that your father's slow and
painful death will be on your head. I
suggest you behave yourself and help with

the arrangements or I'll have to get Ulric
to give you away. Oh, speaking of Ulric,
here is your ring. He really didn't want to
part with it, but I'm always prepared to
please my beloved. Before I go I'm afraid I
have distressing news of the engagement
party. It's been cancelled!" He threw her
father's ring at her and walked out of the
room laughing.

Chapter 27

As the Drakkar sank into the soft earth of
the shore, all the men were on guard. They
needed the ship readily accessible for a
quick escape, so they didn't utilize the
small boats for landing. They knew the way
to the Devorn bastion but did not know the
route to Montfort's. The Viking raiders
couldn't exactly stop by a friendly castle
on the way to ask for directions. Oliver
had supplied them with directions he thought
he remembered, but he didn't know of
Montfort's exact location. Eriik knew they
did not have enough time to be running
around in circles in the English
countryside. He knew of a monastery to the
north and perhaps they could gain some
information there.

"We'll make camp here until the sun rises,
then to the north."

"Aye brother, to the north."

Before the sun rose, the Norsemen were ready
and off doing double time. They all knew
the importance of this journey. This was
not a raid, it was a rescue mission, and
they would not leave without Lady Lillian.
Eriik knew his men. They were warriors and
would fight any army to achieve this for
him. As they made their way to the
monastery, they heard what sounded like
chanting and decided all the priests were
inside for their morning prayers. This
would make it easier to round them all up.
On Eriik's count, they burst into the main

great room as if hell itself had just opened up and all the demons had escaped. The priests were terrified. Eriik and his men had made a shocking entrance. Having their complete attention, Eriik told the priests that they came, not to take treasure or do anyone harm, but for information. One brave soul stood up and came forward, "What information do you seek?"

"We need to find the way to Lord Montfort's fortress."

"To kill and ravage?"

"No, to retrieve what was taken from me and return home in peace. I tell the truth in your Jesus' name."

The priest looked surprised that Eriik knew of Jesus, cocked his head, then slowly told them the way, as much as he could remember. He knew Lord Montfort all too well.

"Thank you father."

"Go with God."

They made good time but were still many miles from their destination, so they made camp for the night and planned to start out again next light. Eriik couldn't get the image of Lillian in Montfort's grasp out of his mind. If he ever got her back into his arms, he would never let her go. Thinking of her always brought his cock to attention. It sprang up strong and demanding, insisting on finding her warm and slick. Oh how he wanted to snuggle up, glide into her, and make sweet love to her again and again. He

swore to himself that would happen very
soon, if she would have him.

Chapter 28

For some reason Lillian had escaped Montfort
the first night and thanked God for it. The
next morning, Millicent, the head of
Montfort's household, came in bright and
enthusiastic, ready to begin the wedding
plans. Lillian decided she had best be
accommodating, lest something awful happen
to her father if it got back to the beast,
as she now thought of Montfort. So she
picked out colors and kinds of cake and a
seamstress came in to measure her for her
wedding dress and incessantly talked about
how much hard work it would take to make
this dress so quickly and how many women it
would take to work on it. Seeming to forget
her place, she curtsied and apologized and
Lillian told her not to give it another
thought. Flowers and food and on and on
until Lillian imagined there couldn't be one
single thing left to decide, when the guest
list was brought up. That took the
remainder of the day. By the time this
farce of a wedding was planned, Lillian was
exhausted and ready to find the bed and fall
to sleep, but was alarmed when Lord Montfort
made an appearance. He closed the door and
approached her much as he did the other
night, reaching for her cheek with his
fingertips. She tried to conceal the
revulsion she felt as he stroked her neck
and shoulders.

"My lord, I thought I made myself perfectly
clear about the bedroom before marriage."

"That was before you tried to run away and I now know it was all a lot of horse dung, wouldn't you say?"

She didn't know if it was the thought of him touching her flesh or what, but she actually felt nauseated.

"My lord, I'm sorry but I don't feel well."

"Don't try to pull that one on me."

He put his hands on her face tight enough to be uncomfortable, leaned in, placing his lips on hers, and she proceeded to throw up in his mouth.

He pulled back, slapped her soundly across the face, coughed and sputtered, then ran from the room.

I'll have to remember that. She laughed.

Throwing up made her feel better but she still felt strange, and decided the best thing would be to try to get some sleep and hope the beast did not come back. Her wish came true.

To her immense pleasure, a maid came in and escorted her back to her chamber. Apparently the lord had not enjoyed her vomit in his mouth. Lillian laughed again. She would be thoroughly enjoying herself if not for the precarious predicament she was in.

The next morning when she awoke, she felt nauseated again and was perplexed, the loathsome lord was nowhere to be seen. She called for the maid, got up, dressed, and waited downstairs for Montfort.

"I would like to see my father please."

"You'll see him when he walks you down the aisle and not before, if you behave yourself, that is. If you don't…"

He jerked her head to one side and looked at his handiwork from the previous night, "You best go back upstairs and apply some powder to your face. We wouldn't want anyone to think my betrothed is clumsy, now would we?"

"You are the lowest of…"

"I wouldn't finish that if I were you and wanted my father to have something to eat this day." He grinned cruelly as he pointed upstairs.

Lillian flew back to the bed chamber, not because of his orders, but because she had to retch again. This was not like her at all. She never got sick. She supposed it was because of the circumstances. Her maid, Alicia, a sweet girl who in the short time Lillian had been there had shown her great kindness, tended to her.

"Are you alright, Miss?"

"Yes I'm fine. I'm sorry."

"No need to be sorry, Miss. I'm just worried about you."

As Lillian tried to be on her way downstairs, she faltered and felt quite dizzy, "Well perhaps I'm not as fine as I proclaimed. Perhaps I'll lie down a bit instead."

Alicia had a funny look on her face as she put a cool cloth on Lillian's face upstairs, "Mum, I don't want to pry, but have you had your time of the month?"

"Don't be silly. You think I'm…no. That's preposterous. Of course I have. It was…"

"Sorry, it's just you have all the symptoms. I'm sorry to have been out of line."

"Not at all. Thank you for your concern Alicia. I appreciate your help."

After Alicia left the room, Lillian tried to think when her time of the month had come. With all that was happening, she hadn't noticed, but since Alicia mentioned it, she just realized it had *not* come this month. Could it be? No, it was absurd. Or was it? She had been feeling nauseated, but she put that squarely at the feet of Lord Montfort, after all he could make her queasy just looking at him. Even so, her bouts of dizziness weren't like her either. She put her hands on her belly and wondered if it was possible a little Eriik could be sheltered there. Was she happy if it were so? What a hellish predicament she was in if it was true. What would she do? If she were destined to marry the beast, would she pawn Eriik's child off as his? That would be unthinkable. If she ran away, her father's fate would be sealed. She prayed with all her strength for God to help her. It looked as if He might be the only one who could.

Catherine Sharp
Viking's Desire161

Chapter 29

Eriik's men were traveling fast. As they
prepared camp, he picked a few men to scout
out what was ahead. They had to be sure
Montfort was the lord of the manor the
priest described before they attacked the
bastion. Perhaps there was a village or a
church nearby where they could get some
information. At first light some of the men
would march out and hopefully return with
good news. Eriik taught all of them two
sentences in English. *Where is Lord
Montfort's fortress? I'll pay you in gold.*
He was upset about wasting so much time but
didn't want to get involved in an attack on
the wrong stronghold. He prayed over and
over again to the gods to keep Lillian safe
until he could get to her. Perhaps she
could feel him near. *I'm coming for you
sweet.*

His men returned and they had the news he
was waiting for. They were indeed on the
right path to Montfort's. They had to pay
more gold than he wanted for the information
but in the end it was worth it. Eriik
couldn't think of a better way to spend his
fortune. The men started out again. At
camp, they knew this would be the last night
before battle, so every man tended to their
weapons as they would a lover. Their
weapons were their lives or deaths. Each
man was ready.

Sol was starting his ride across the heavens
when Eriik and his men were on the move

again. They should arrive at their destination before nightfall. Eriik couldn't travel fast enough. With every step, he could feel Lillian's heart beat stronger. As he spotted the fortress in the distance, he could almost see Lillian with her beautiful face and emerald green orbs looking at him with desire and long dark locks spilling down her back like a sable waterfall. He was painfully hard again. Only Lillian could do this to his body without so much as a look or a touch. She was his undoing and he loved every wonderful, agonizing moment of it. Enough of this daydreaming. He had to get his mind back on the battlefield and off of the bed chamber or Montfort might win and the thought of that was inconceivable. This battle was different from all the rest. He had no intention of dying in battle and going to Valhalla willingly. That would leave his lovely Lillian in the hands of the depraved Montfort, so this battle would have to be won, at any cost.

As they marched on, the sentries of the castle spotted the invaders and called out a warning to all inside the castle. Simon had not expected this at all. He ran to the wall to see for himself. A voyage from afar from this heathen for Lillian? He underestimated this Jarl's feelings for her, but he would not be fighting this behemoth. There would be no bloodshed, especially if it might be his own. He rushed up the stairs to confront Lillian. He would insist she diffuse this and do so immediately. He practically crashed through her door looking completely terrified. Seeing him in such a state gave her some satisfaction, although she had no idea what had put the fear of God into him.

"What in the world, my lord? You look as if you've seen a ghost."

"You're whore hound is sniffing about. I can't believe it, but I went up to the wall and saw for myself."

"Eriik?" She ran to the window, searching the landscape, trying to spy him. Finally she saw what looked like many men marching toward the castle.

"Oh my God."

"Yes, you'll be calling for your God when I get finished with your father. If you think this pagan will save you, just remember what fate your father faces if anything happens to one hair on my head."

Her heart sank as she realized that nothing had changed. Well, except one thing, Eriik loved her. Eriik really loved her!

"This is what is going to happen and what you are going to do. Listen carefully sweet pea," he said with disdain.

"I will send an emissary out as soon as your lover arrives and invite him in."

At the look of pure fear on her face he continued, "Don't worry my little whore, he won't be hurt, because you are going to be quite convincing as you tell him you are very much in love with me and can't wait to be blissfully married. Do you understand?

I can't afford to kill him and have his hoards attack. I'm not stupid."

She said nothing as her throat constricted with tears, but nodded her assent.

"There, there, that's my good girl."

She turned her back to him. She simply couldn't face him.

How could she let Eriik know what was really going on?

She had concluded that she was indeed with child, Eriik's child. She was so afraid that if Simon found out, he would beat her until she lost the child, if not her own life. He seemed to always be on the verge of beating her anyway, she could only imagine how enraged he would be if he found out she was carrying Eriik's child

Chapter 30

Eriik couldn't sleep at all that night. He
wanted so badly to attack the devil's
fortress and take his Lillian back into his
arms, but he couldn't let his emotions get
the best of him. Everything had to go as
planned, as every other battle or Lillian
might get hurt. At dawn, as expected, a
rider appeared from the castle, riding out
to the halfway position between the fortress
and Eriik's men. He was in his chain mail
and rode a magnificent charger with another
fine steed trailing behind. He stood there
waiting for Eriik. Bjorn advised Eriik
against the meeting, "What if this is an
ambush and it's their way of getting rid of
our leader right at the beginning?"

"Then they are quite the fool. Our men
would charge the castle, rescue Lillian, and
everyone's life would be at stake inside and
he knows it full well. He may be a devil,
but he's no idiot, and neither am I. This
isn't the first time I've done this. I'll
be on my guard and you're coming with me.
This is exactly what we expected after all,
yes?"

"Yes."

Every archer, among Eriik's men, were on
guard with arrows at the ready for any sign
of trouble. Bjorn, Eriik and the knight met
in the middle of the field and stated their
business. Eriik minced no words, putting it
very simply as soon as he was within earshot

of Lord Montfort's knight, "I want the Lady Lillian in my camp immediately…unharmed."

The knight retorted, "That's impossible sir, she and Lord Montfort are engaged to be married. She is indeed unharmed and Lord Montfort has empowered me to invite you to the castle to see for yourself that the lady is not only safe but happy and looking forward to the upcoming nuptials. You have his word on your safety, but he will not tolerate any raucous behavior."

Eriik snorted and said under his breath, "His word," but said aloud, "I agree."

"But brother…"

"Nay Bjorn, I must see for myself."

Bjorn turned his attention to the knight, "Then come back with another horse for me. The Jarl will not enter the enemy's abode alone."

The knight turned both steeds around and rode the way he had come, as Eriik and Bjorn returned to camp.

Bjorn looked at Eriik as if he was a lunatic, "I know you love her, but this is not a wise act. Dammit! I can already tell you won't be dissuaded. I can see it in your eyes, so if you insist, I have your back, whatever the outcome."

"Thank you brother."

When the knight returned he had two horses trailing behind and once again Eriik and Bjorn met him on the field. They mounted and rode toward the enemy willingly. He was finally going to see Lillian. She couldn't be there of her own accord. He would make sure they left together.

As they entered the great room of the cold and soulless castle, Lord Montfort and Lillian were descending the stairway. Eriik could read the terror in Montfort's eyes just by looking at him. He had his hand held out for Lillian's and her hand rested gently upon his cold, slight fingers. Eriik noticed that his thin, feeble arms looked more like a scarecrow's than a living, breathing man.

Lillian tried not to but found herself looking squarely into sea blue orbs, noticed the torment outlining his face, and could feel his agony. He was so male, pure heat, with his huge, strong arms, bristling with hard, corded muscle encased by golden arm bands that matched his thick golden hair. If only she could run her fingers through it once again and take the pain from his beautiful blue eyes. He stood with his legs apart, his hard muscles tense, waiting to spring into action as a predator waiting for its prey.

Instead she said as detached and as coolly as she possibly could, "Good evening Eriik."

Eriik laughed a vicious laugh, "Good evening Eriik? Is that all you have to say to me? You're standing there with your hand touching that viper's flesh and seemingly content. What's the matter with you Lillian? Tell me!"

"I don't know what you're talking about. I'm about to become a Lady of the Realm, quite impressive, don't you think? Believe me, many women would love to trade places with me."

"Then trade."

Lord Montfort broke in, "I say sir, I believe I've been insulted quite enough in my own home and I'll have no more of it. I have been quite hospitable to you and you're, uh friends. I will have to ask you to at least try to act like a gentlemen, if nothing more."

"Montfort, I'll have a word with Lillian in private."

"You will have nothing of the sort. My betrothed alone with another man is completely improper. You may say whatever you will here and now and then you may go back to wherever you came from. Simon looked at Lillian with the strangest look Eriik had ever seen and Lillian looked back at him with an equally peculiar expression, as if they were sharing secrets. He couldn't understand this at all! She despised the vermin and now she was standing here as if he was her great love and she couldn't wait to marry him. The world was turning upside down and Eriik didn't know how to stop it. She stood there regally and asked, "Is there anything else you'd care to know?"

"Lillian, what has happened to you?"

"Nothing. I'm quite happy, really. I'm at home, planning the wedding of the season with my father and as you know, it was the wish of my dearly departed mother. What in the world do you mean, happened to me?"

"You can tell me the truth."

"Oh my lord, there are so many truths."

"What in hell does that…" He stopped short as he noticed a bruise under her left eye covered by powder. He tried his best to leash in the uncontrollable rage that was enveloping him.

"He hit you?"

"Of course not, I'm just clumsy and fell."

Montfort interjected, "I would never…"

"Why in the name of your god are you covering for him? Tell me what happened."

Before she could stop herself, she sighed, "Oh if only I could."

"What? What!"

"I was just prattling on. You know nerves about the wedding. All of a sudden, she felt faint and reached for the stair rail to steady herself, and at the same time reached protectively for her belly. The feeling passed in a moment and she apologized, but Eriik couldn't shake the uneasy feeling that small gesture produced. He couldn't put his finger on it, but it unsettled him. Lillian had such an odd expression on her face, it took Eriik completely aback. He didn't know

exactly why, but he was determined to find
out.

Lillian smiled almost shyly, "My Lord
Thorennson, I appreciate your concern for my
well-being, but I really must be attending
to other pressing engagements. I have so
many plans and decisions to make, for the
wedding of course. You understand, don't
you?"

"Not really. But I will, you can count on
it. By the way, I haven't seen your father,
where is he? I would have thought he would
be here for the happy occasion." Eriik
couldn't control the bite in his words.

The shocked look on Lillian's face told a
tale, he wasn't sure what it was but he had
a strong suspicion it wasn't a fairytale.
He had the distinct feeling that something
was hiding behind those emerald eyes.
Everything was definitely not right in this
household and he was not leaving until he
knew what it was.

"Well, it appears I, we, came a long way for
nothing, however since it was such a long
journey, I must insist you do me the honor
of inviting me to the pre-wedding feast."

As Montfort opened his mouth to speak,
Lillian interrupted immediately, "Of course,
that's the least we can do."

After much stuttering and stammering,
Montfort added, "I suppose that could be
arranged." He certainly didn't appear
pleased with the proposition of having these
giants of men playing guests at his table.

"You must not scare any of our genteel guests however, and you must give me your word this will be the end of it. You will leave, never to bother us again."

"I'll try not to behead anyone before dessert, if that's what you mean." Eriik almost snarled as he tried to speak politely to the man he could hardly stand to be in the same room with.

"Very funny, Jarl. You know exactly what I mean. Afterwards, you'll be gone and back to wherever you come from.

"Aye. Just a dinner to see Lillian off to married bliss, yes?"

"Fine. Now we both have much to do. Is that all?"

For some reason Eriik needed to know about Lillian's father, "I assume I'll see Lord Devorn at the festivities?"

"Yes I'm sure you will." Montfort interjected before Lillian had a chance to speak. "You know he's not one of your biggest fans."

"No, I'm sure he's not." Eriik added as he veered away and started to leave.

"Until then," Montfort snorted derisively, turned his back, and led Lillian upstairs.

****

As Eriik and Bjorn rode back to camp, most of what she had said rang in his ears. All he could think about was her small dainty hand resting gracefully on that vermin's. Everything looked fine, but he still couldn't shake the strong feeling that it wasn't. Could it feasibly have been a little too right, perhaps as if it was staged? And the way she looked at him, so strangely after she faltered. Was he trying to find an explanation for something too bizarre for his mind to accept? What could she possibly gain by pretending? If he was threatening her, she could have run to him then and there. Thinking about their meeting and the strange things she said was making him more confused, not less. Dammit! What was hiding just beyond his grasp?

Bjorn was very vocal about Eriik being crazy to put himself in danger to attend the wedding feast.

"Why would you even want to go to the sodding feast, that's what I don't understand? Obviously Lillian has decided to marry that despicable man for money, land, and politics. Apparently you didn't know her as well as you thought you did. Eriik, I know you think this is the end of the world, and I admit you will be upset for a bit, but as soon as we get home, there are so many temptations waiting for you there that will eventually help you forget. One very beautiful young lady I know of is absolutely determined to make you erase Lillian from your memory entirely. I'm sure she has some very amorous ideas of how to go about it. By the gods, it sends my blood racing. Just let her have her way and you'll see it will happen."

"You're probably right, my friend."

Perhaps Bjorn was right but all Eriik could think of was dark hair, fair skin, emerald green eyes, soft breasts, and welcoming legs opening to beckon him into her soft warmth.

Chapter 31

The wedding plans continued and the fear
kept mounting as Lillian was trapped in an
unconscionable situation. Perhaps if she
escaped to Eriik's camp and told him
everything, he could somehow save her father
and they could be together after all.
Perhaps and somehow didn't make her feel all
that confident. If she ran to Eriik and her
father died, she would never forgive
herself. On the other hand, she couldn't
marry the vicious Lord Montfort, even if she
wasn't with child, but she certainly
couldn't go forward with it carrying Eriik's
child. What in the world could she do?

This is what she felt like the night before
she walked down the stairs to Eriik so many
months ago. It had been traumatic then but
somehow not so much as now. She felt as if
her life was over then too, but she fell in
love with Eriik instead. Could she be that
lucky a second time and a miracle save her
again? She decided to go on with the
wedding feast before trying to make a
decision. Her father would be there and
perhaps she could come up with some way for
them both to escape unharmed. Her head was
constantly spinning with ideas, making for
quite the headache. She felt dizzy again,
so with Alicia's help, she changed and
decided to lie down for awhile. Before she
could get any rest, Simon burst into the

room, shooed Alicia out, and sat by her side on the bed.

"My dear, we need to have a little talk."

Lillian looked at him apprehensively but didn't say a word.

"I'm sure you're thinking of all sorts of ways to try to escape to your lover, somehow leaving your father unharmed, and I've come to put those silly notions out of that pretty head of yours. You see, I will be placing my best archers in the struts of the great room, with their arrows aimed straight for the heart of the Jarl and your father, should you say or act the slightest bit odd. Therefore, you will act the part of the perfect bride to be, do you understand?"

She couldn't stop the shocked look on her face.

"Yes, just as I expected. Your scheming, conniving ways are very evident. Do you think I'm a complete idiot?"

"No, I, uh…"

"Stop it now. Just tell me what a good girl you will be and I'll leave you to your rest."

"Yes my lord, I won't do anything to upset you, I swear."

"Yes, you better swear, on your father's life."

"Not only do I expect you not to do something strange, I expect you to smile and

laugh and be the loving bride to be." He
stressed loving as he sauntered out with an
evil grin on his cruel face. He acted as if
he was enjoying himself.

Chapter 32

Everyone was gathering in the great room,
festive with wedding decorations. The
servants had outdone themselves at Lord
Montfort's orders. Great succulent slabs of
pork, beef, goat, pheasant, and chicken on
great trenchers were being served with so
many huge containers of fruits and
vegetables, one couldn't count. There were
a variety of sweets with their fragrant,
appetizing aromas escaping from the kitchen,
teasing the guests palate, waiting to be
served later. Jugglers, musicians,
wrestlers, and songsters entertained the
guests and no one, except Eriik, who had
been observing the revelry attentively,
would have ever been able to guess that
anything sinister was going on. It looked
to be nothing short of pure joy, but Eriik
couldn't help but believe that something
else was afoot. As Eriik and Bjorn were
being seated, he beheld the most exquisite
vision he'd ever had the pleasure of gazing
upon, as Lillian gracefully descended the
stairway in a gorgeous cream colored
creation of silk and lace, with a
décolletage low enough to catch just a
glimpse of the cleavage of her soft,
flawless breasts. Eriik was glad he was
seated so no one could see how hard he was
becoming, simply catching sight of his
lovely Lillian. He couldn't really call her
his now, could he? He noticed many other
gentlemen acting quite the same way and an
unreasonable stab of jealousy hit him hard.
It took every ounce of strength he had not

to jump up and take their heads off right then and there. She reached the chairs and with grace and elegance took her seat at the head of the table, and not for the first time put her hand protectively on her belly just for a second, but he was watching her so closely, a second was all he needed to notice. This was not the first time, and he found it to be quite peculiar, but thought no more of it as he couldn't take his eyes off the bounty of her beauty. It brought him nothing but pain, both physical and emotional. Just for a moment, emerald green and sea blue eyes met, then she looked away quickly. Why wouldn't she meet him eye to eye?

As Lord Montfort entered the room, everyone, excepting Eriik and Bjorn stood and clapped, shouting congratulations to the bride and groom. Lillian rose and met him with open arms and a smile on her face. Eriik couldn't believe his eyes, even though he was looking straight at her. She looked happy. How could she have lied so convincingly when she was with him? Had the whole time been one big lie for her, just waiting to escape? He was not only full of pain but rage as well. At this point he was sorry he had insisted they attend the feast, all he wanted to do was get out of there and journey home as fast as their ship could take them. He didn't know how much more of this he could take without ripping someone apart, or being ripped apart himself from the inside out. He could only hope he was keeping his emotions to himself. It was then he spotted Lord Devorn being escorted to sit beside Lillian. He seemed frail and

gaunt, and why was he being lead to his
seat? Was he ill? He had no more time to
think about it as Montfort leaned over to
kiss Lillian on the cheek and she actually
seemed to beam at him, or if not, she was
one hell of an actress. Oh by the gods, he
wanted to jump over the tables and tear
Montfort to shreds.

The night seemed to go on an eternity until
finally Eriik and Bjorn could rise, pretend
to thank their hosts, and leave.

Lillian was watching Eriik, the pain etched
clearly on his handsome face, watching him
walk out of the room and out of her
life...forever. The frozen smile on her face
hid the desolation she felt. Everything in
her wanted to scream for him to stay, to
take her with him, that she loved him. But
she remained quietly frozen in place.

Chapter 33

As Eriik and Bjorn reached their campsite,
Eriik bellowed as loud as he could,
"Brothers, we break camp at dawn, to the
ships, and back home!"

A cheer went up. It seemed to Eriik that
all the men were as ready as he was to be
away from this Saxon land. Dawn couldn't
come fast enough for him. He was looking
forward to feeling the cold spray of the sea
in his face. He needed to feel his muscles
strain with the pull of the huge oars. He
was going home. As he stared at the
stunning display of stars dotting the night
sky like jewels, he saw, not for the first
time, Renouf sneaking off for the fortress,
and he couldn't help but smile. At least
someone was tossing up a skirt. He knew he
should stop and chastise him. It was, after
all, a bit dangerous, but he was a big boy
and could take care of himself. Eriik
wondered who the English wench was and hoped
she didn't get Renouf in trouble. As long
as he was back by dawn, Eriik shook his head
and decided to let it be. Freya, the
goddess of love, would have to look out for
the lucky lad tonight.

****

Eriik and his men started breaking camp at
dawn and he noticed that Renouf was not
among them.

He hoped he had not been foolhardy with his
decision to let him go on to the fortress

for reasons of the flesh. Eriik could not
wait around for the young man to return
because Renouf had let his randy side get
the best of him. He would have to catch up
with them on his own. Surely he hadn't
decided to stay. He couldn't even speak the
language. He briefly wondered how he
communicated with the young lady. Flesh to
flesh he guessed and laughed out loud.
Bjorn looked at him questioningly and Eriik
asked him, "Have you noticed that Renouf
isn't here?"

"Aye yes, he has a young lady at the house."

"I hope he knows what he's gotten into."

"I think that's all he knows."

They both laughed as they started the long
trek back to the ship. Laughing felt good
after the previous evening.

This was the first part of the journey home
and that felt good too.

After a couple of hours, Eriik's keen
hearing picked up hoof beats coming toward
them at a rapid speed.

He motioned toward the sound of the horse,
"Men, be ready."

All the men were prepared when over the rise
they saw Renouf riding fast with his young
lady balanced in front of him. Eriik's men
relaxed and put their weapons down. As
Renouf brought the horse to a halt, Eriik
asked the young man sternly, "Renouf, what
in hell do you think you're doing? Stealing

a horse and bringing your lady here. You've got a lot of explaining to do and I suspect you should be quick about it. We've got a lot of ground to cover and I'm anxious to get started home."

"My lord, I can't really explain it…"

Eriik exploded, "Can't explain it!"

"Wait a minute and let me tell you what I know. Alicia has been prattling away for the last hour and as you know, I can't understand a word of what she says, but she keeps fearfully grabbing me and talking about the lady Lillian. She wouldn't let me leave this morning without her and before I knew it, she had the horse saddled and, well, here we are."

"Alicia, you say?"

Alicia interrupted at the mention of her name, "Aye my lord. I understand you speak English?"

"That is so young lady. Now what is all this about?"

"My lord, Lady Lillian is with child."

Eriik's face went as white as a snow covered peak.

"Thank you for apprising me of the happy couple's good news. Why in the world would you come here to tell me this? Did Montfort put you up to it?"

"Oh my lord, no you don't understand, I can't let you leave without telling you the truth of what injustice is being dealt to the lady Lillian."

"The lady has made it quite clear…"

"No!" Alicia interrupted again, "You do not know what you speak of. The lady is being forced to play the happy bride to be."

"Forced, how?"

"Her father is being held captive, his life in danger if she does or says anything disobedient to Lord Montfort. He will kill Lord Devorn if she doesn't obey him absolutely."

"Why would you endanger your own life to bring me this information?"

"Lady Lillian has been very kind to me and Lord Montfort is, well, to say he is not kind would be treating his wickedness lightly. He is a cruel and sadistic man and the lady spending her life with him, especially carrying *your* child would be a travesty."

"What lass? Carrying whose child?"

"Yes, of course it is your child. Think about it, she hasn't been here that long and I know for a fact the lady has not shared the lord's bed. The child is yours."

Her hand protectively on her belly.

"Mine!" Eriik bellowed like an angry bear. After allowing himself a moment to settle down, he asked a little less violently, "This is a fact?"

"Yes, my lord."

"Where is her father being held?"

"In the cellar below the stairs where prisoners are kept. He has guards twenty four hours a day with orders to kill him if there is any escape attempt on her part. Lady Lillian is beside herself with worry."

"Thank you Alicia. You will not return, in case someone has noticed your leaving. It's too dangerous."

After some consideration, he continued, "What would you think of returning to our land with us?"

"With the lady Lillian?"

"Aye. As long as I have breath in my body, I will not leave this land without her safely in my arms!"

"Yes, yes." She looked shyly at Renouf, who looked on in complete ignorance.

Eriik smiled, "You are welcome in my household, Alicia, always."

"Thank you my lord."

Eriik explained all that had transpired to his men.

"This is not something I'm commanding of you, it's absolutely voluntary. You are free to go back to the ship with my blessing and no hard feelings. You've already come this far for me for personal reasons. You need not go any further. Aye or nay."

Each and every man raised their weapons above their heads, "Aye!"

Eriik smiled, "Brothers, we have a lot of planning to do."

Chapter 34

After breakfast the next morning, Lord
Montfort held his hand out, expecting
Lillian to take it gracefully, however she
only looked at him with contempt.

"Don't make a scene, I'll be escorting you
to your chambers without incident," he
whispered.

"The only person I wish to escort me to my
chambers is my father."

"I'm afraid he's tied up at the moment." He
laughed at his own joke and took her hand,
even as she tried to jerk it back.

"If you're not careful dear you'll be
sleeping down there with him."

"Oh, you pig!"

"Shh, you little slut. I won't have a
commotion where the help can see or hear,
but if you think I won't make you pay when
we're alone, then you better think again.
Now behave yourself or you'll be sore
tomorrow."

"You mean sorry?"

"I mean sore."

"You wouldn't."

"Oh, but I would, and I'll enjoy it too, but
even more so I'll be giving instructions for
your father to be beaten as well. He's on
the frail side these days so he might not be

able to stand a good beating. I guess we'll have to see."

"No, no. I'm sorry my lord. I mean no disrespect. I'll accompany you happily to my chambers, as you wish."

"Now that is a good girl. I knew I could convince you to be reasonable. Come along. We'll speak of our upcoming nuptials as we walk. You are excited about them, as any young bride would be, yes?"

"Yes my lord."

Lillian blinked back tears as they walked. She didn't know what Simon would do if he noticed, but she didn't care to find out. Eriik was gone and she was left here to marry the most horrible man she had ever met and try to pass Eriik's son or daughter off as his. The thought of it was sickening. What fate he or she would meet was too horrible to contemplate, especially if it was born with beautiful golden hair. Even if Montfort thought the child was his, she couldn't imagine him being anything but a horrid father. Perhaps he would just ignore the boy or girl, as did most lords with their offspring. That would be the best future she could hope for her son or daughter. She prayed the child would have her hair color. She had no misconceptions about what would happen otherwise. At the door of her chamber, she turned to Simon and politely said, "Thank you, I believe I'll lie down awhile. I'm still a bit tired from last eve."

"Yes, it was a trying evening. I would insist on staying in your chamber this morning since you're planning to be in bed anyway, but that will happen soon enough, so I'll take my leave, I have so much planning to do. Remember Lady Lillian, very soon you will be in my chamber. Don't forget it."

She closed the door and tears streamed down her cheeks. She tiredly slipped into bed wondering how she could go on with her life with the repugnant lord beside her night after night. And worse still, not just beside her. She prayed for a miracle and then cried herself to sleep.

Chapter 35

Eriik and his men slipped far enough away to
be out of sight, but still close enough to
pull off a rescue. All day, Eriik and his
advisors devised plan after plan of how to
steal into the castle, not only taking
Lillian and Lord Devorn out unharmed, but
without causing a major battle. Eriik was
afraid if a battle became necessary, Lillian
or her father would get hurt and that was
not an option.

"Renouf, get Alicia, perhaps she can advise
us on this. She knows the place far better
than we do."

Renouf returned with an eager Alicia, not
quite sure of what she was there for, but
ready to help in any way she could.

"My lord?"

"Alicia, we are at a standstill as how to
rescue Lord Devorn and Lady Lillian without
waking the gods and bringing a full battle
down upon our heads. We were hoping you
could tell us something we could use before
Renouf escorts you back to the ship in the
morning."

"Back to the ship?"

"Aye. It's far too dangerous for you here.

"My lord, with due respect, I'll be doing no
such thing. I can give you just so much
information, but without me there to show
you, you'll get nowhere. I certainly can't

tell you how to open the door from the
tunnel or under the stairs for that matter,
or even how to find it. It's hidden quite
well. You'll be hunting it for hours. I
must go with you.

"That will put your life in danger, Alicia."

"Then so be it, I must go with you for there
to be any chance to save my lady and her
father. Have you thought what would happen
to your child raised in that house? What if
it's born with golden hair? You best be
sensible and include me in your plans."

"You're truly a brave girl. Alright then,
explain what you can, we'll settle on a plan
and Renouf will be by your side every step
of the way, understood?"

"Yes, my lord." Eriik could tell Alicia
didn't mind that part of the plan one bit.

After Alicia told them every detail she
could, Renouf escorted her back to his tent
and in broken English Eriik had taught him,
told her to get some rest. They would move
that night.

There was only one way into the house
besides the main gate. It was an escape
tunnel for the nobles if there was a siege
upon the castle. It was well hidden inside
the walls and no one was supposed to know
where to find it but the family, in this
case, Lord Montfort. He hadn't even told
his cousin, James, however, Theona knew
where it was so she could keep it clear of
debris. He was terrified after Castle
Devorn had been taken that he would not have

an escape if needed and always made sure the
tunnel was kept unobstructed. Theona was
sworn to secrecy with death being the
punishment. She told Alicia anyway in case
she ever needed it. Alicia tried to talk
her into escaping the horrible lord many
times, knowing how he treated her, but it
was to no avail.

Alicia would have to go first to the door
from the tunnel to the castle since it was
quite tricky to open. The tunnel was only
large enough for one man at a time, so
Eriik, Bjorn, and Renouf would follow single
file. If a fight broke out upon entering
the castle, their men would be outside,
having stolen unseen to the front wall,
swords at the ready, hoping one of the three
inside could make it to the gate and get it
open in time for them to enter. They hoped
that would not be necessary.

When the time came, Alicia and the three men
slipped to the tunnel hidden well in the
shrubbery. They would never have found it
without her. It was a tight fit for the
men, but Alicia ran through it quickly,
having the door open when the men arrived.
They went directly to the hatch hidden well,
under the rug in the floor at the stairs.
They knew they must free Lord Devorn first
in order to convince Lady Lillian to make
the escape with them. They were concerned
that without her father, she would go
nowhere, fearing for his life. Alicia knew
how to open the intricate latch on the trap
door because she had taken the lord and his
captors food many times. After the latch
was open, Alicia was sent back to camp, out

of harm's way. Eriik didn't want to have to worry about her, along with everyone else. As Bjorn and Eriik descended the stairs, they saw Lord Devorn chained to a chair and the three priests, or rather thugs they recognized from the missionary group, armed, guarding him.

"Yield and there will be no bloodshed. I've come for Lord Devorn, even though I would take great pleasure in drawing first blood for my Lady Lillian, stand down and live."

"There will be no yielding pagan, Ulric had his sword in hand and swung for Eriik's head, but Eriik stepped aside and struck Ulric's sword. Lunge and parry again and again until a final surge from Eriik and he struck Ulric downward from shoulder to groin. As blood ran from Ulric's mouth, the sense of what had happened sunk in, and he would say no more.

The other two, who had been at a stand-off with Bjorn and Renouff threw their swords down, knelt, and yielded. After they were chained and gagged, Eriik was concerned, "Bjorn, this is taking too much time and we're making too much noise. I will finish down here, you and Renouf get the gate open."

"Aye."

As Eriik started for Lillian's chamber, as described by Alicia, he stopped dead in his tracks and looked on horrified as Lillian was standing on the stairway with Montfort behind her holding a deadly looking knife to her graceful throat.

"I had a bad feeling when Millicent apprised me of the commotion downstairs. Why can't you just leave us alone, or better yet, just die! I can't seem to find Lady Lillian's hand maiden. Is she the bitch who betrayed me? When I see her again, I'll make certain her smile is bloody from ear to ear."

Eriik slowly, calmly, pulled out his bow and placed an arrow in the arrow rest.

"Montfort, I swear…"

"You swear what, Jarl? If you lob that arrow, you might hit me, probably not fatally, but you'll definitely hit the lady. Now do you really want to take that chance?"

"Are you such a suckling coward that you cannot face me man to man, you must hide behind a woman's skirts?"

"Oh say what you must, I know that you will not hurt me as long as I have this knife to her pretty flesh, and furthermore, we will be leaving together unharmed. Command your dogs to stay until our carriage is away and she will live."

"You expect me to take your word for that? Besides, I will never leave her in your hands, never!

Lillian, are you alright?"

"Eriik, just kill him, please."

"Oh, this is quite amusing, you two. How charming how the maiden kidnapped by the big bad wolf fell madly in love with him. Why

that's simply charming. What fairy tales
are made of really."

Eriik's men came charging through the gates
and stopped at his command and about the
same time, Montfort's knights arrived ready
to fight, stopping in mid stride to gape at
the sight of Lord Montfort holding his lady
at knifepoint.

"Well what are you waiting for, kill them."
Montfort yelled.

Eriik, still holding his bow, said loudly
for all his men and Montfort's knights to
hear, "My men will stand down. We are only
here for Lady Lillian. Ask her yourself if
she wants to stay with Montfort, or if she
wishes to come with me, and ask yourself,
why is your lord holding a knife to her
throat? I wish no man here any injury as
long as the lady remains unharmed."

One of the knights stepped forward and
asked, "Lady Lillian, what are your wishes?"

"Sir Knight, I wish to go with Lord
Thorennson!"

Montfort brought the knife closer to
Lillian's throat and a fine trickle of blood
ran slowly down her throat between her
breasts. Eriik was enraged.

The knight took a step back looking
dismayed.

"Montfort, if you hurt her, I will flay you
like a fish, every slice while you're awake

to feel the knife slice through your flesh.
I do not speak idly, I swear!"

"Well, we're at quite an impasse. Let me
leave unharmed and everyone will be fine,
including the lady."

Just at that moment Lillian faltered,
looking as if she would faint, and for just
an instant it gave Eriik the target he
needed, as he already had the arrow at the
ready. He let the arrow fly straight and
true, exact, right through Montfort's eye.
All Montfort had time to do was utter a
short shriek as he feel backward onto the
stairs. He didn't have time to take Lillian
with him as Eriik was already at her side,
catching her in his embrace. The men in the
great hall facing each other really didn't
know what to do. They were enemies, they
should be fighting, however the lady and the
Norse leader were in each other's arms.

From quite out of nowhere, an unfamiliar
voice rang out.

"I am Lord Regent James Montfort. Regent
Lord only until the King approves my title.
There will be no bloodshed inside these
walls or on my land. I can see quite
clearly that Lady Lillian has been held here
against her wishes by my cousin and will be
leaving soon with our guest?"

"Jarl of Jaedon, Eriik Thorennson at your
service."

"Yes, of course."

James Montfort looked at his knights still standing at the ready, "Sir William?"

"My lord. You know my name?"

"Yes, Simon convinced all of you I was a half-wit and I played along, otherwise I may very well be dead by now, but I know all of your names. It's a shame he didn't value you as I do. Please gather several men to take a message to the king to advise him that Lord Simon Montfort was taken from us too soon in a tragic hunting accident. I'll pen the letter and seal it."

"Yes my lord."

"Lord Thorennson and Lady Lillian, I do apologize for not being able to offer you much hospitality after this horrific affair but I do have a funeral to plan, however you are welcome to stay as long as you wish before returning home. The staff will show you all the hospitality you were not afforded previously."

"Thank you Lord Montfort, but the lady and I will see her father home and then my men and I will also be returning home."

"I can certainly understand your haste in wishing to return so soon. I can only apologize for my cousin and I hope you accept it. I am quite sincere."

Lillian placed a soft kiss on James' cheek, "Simon was an evil man but it was his doing and no one else's, certainly not yours."

"Thank you Lady Lillian for your graciousness. May God be with you. Good travels."

Eriik, Lillian, her father, and Eriik's men turned and marched out of Montfort castle.

Eriik turned to Lord Devorn, "Lord, I must break my word I made to you last we met. I vowed to never walk on your land again, and now I must, in order to take you home."

"Eriik Thorennson, you are welcome on my land anytime," Frederick laughed and hugged his daughter.

Lillian looked at Eriik seriously, "You told James Montfort that you and your men would be returning home."

"Aye."

"Is that everyone?"

With a gleam in his eye, "Is there someone else who would like to go? I would never presume to force anyone. It would have to be their choice."

"You're going to make me say it, aren't you?"

"Aye."

Lillian blushed an attractive pink, "Yes, you oaf, I want to go home with you."

"Home?" Eriik questioned.

"Home." Lillian was radiant.

Eriik swung her up in his arms and hugged her so tight she thought she might break, but she had never been happier.

When they arrived back at their camp, all was packed and ready to go in no time. Eriik called Alicia to him and told her all the events that happened inside the walls after she left and explained to Lillian what Alicia had done to bring them back together.

Lillian hugged her in a warm embrace, "How can I ever repay you? You saved my life, well actually two lives." She whispered in her ear as she cradled her still flat belly lovingly.

Eriik chimed in, "Alicia, you will always have an honored place in my, our household, but I'm sure you will be safe here as well if you wish to stay. It's a long and difficult voyage. Our land is harsh, our winters cold. I want you to know what you're getting yourself into. It's your choice."

Alicia didn't hesitate, "I wish to come with you."

"Then let's get started. Lord Devorn, you are also welcome to come with us to be with your daughter."

"Thank you, but no. I'm too old and my home is here. I would love to be with my daughter and see my grandchildren but I need to stay."

"Then we'll come back here to see you, not to do any mischief mind you. I can't promise the same from the young ones we'll be bringing with us however, but I will just be paying a visit, if I'm still welcome," Eriik grinned.

"More than welcome."

It was difficult for Lillian to say good bye to her father, but she knew her place was with Eriik and she looked forward to her new life by his side, no pretending, no lies, just honestly loving him. She had a secret she needed to tell him soon or she wouldn't need to, he would be able to see for himself, but it wasn't something she could just blurt out. She needed a special time when they could be alone. They stopped for a break just a couple of hours from the ship. Just the two of them, sitting on an outcropping of rocks separated from the rest of the men, Alicia nowhere to be seen. Lillian took Eriik's hand and looked deeply into his deep sea blue eyes, "Eriik, I have the most wonderful news, I, uh…"

"Do you think it's a boy or a girl?"

"A, what?"

"I'm sorry, I should have let you tell me, but I already knew, sweet. Yes, it is the most wonderful news."

"But how?"

"As I told you, Alicia risked her life to sneak out to tell me you were pretending to be in love with that villainous creature to save your father's life. She told me you were carrying my child and thought it would be nothing short of immoral for me not to know, you being abandoned to live with that creature, and me thinking you were in love with him."

"Oh thank goodness for Alicia."

"I second that." He sealed it with a searing kiss.

Chapter 36

This time on the ship, they slept quite
nicely together, cuddling for each other's
warmth and knowing they would never be
complete without the other. The journey
wasn't at all as tedious as the one before.
When land was called this time, Lillian was
looking forward to being *home*.

As they set foot on solid ground, Eriik was
pleased to see his kinsmen and people from
the village receive Lillian with eager cries
of welcome. They were glad to see her and
it did his heart good. Lillian's eyes were
full as she now considered these people her
own. Eriik didn't need a wagon to take his
treasure home from this journey, the most
valuable treasure in the world was holding
his hand and walking happily with him. As
they neared his keep, he swept Lillian up
into his arms and carried her across the
threshold, "Welcome to my, uh, our home,
sweet. This is how you should have entered
the house of Thorennson in the beginning my
lady, and I'm truly sorry you did not. I
never explained to you the why of it all and
you deserve more. I fell in love with you
the first moment I laid eyes on your beauty
and I selfishly had to have you. I can't
say I'm sorry because if I had not, you
wouldn't be here now, but I am sorry the
tortures you suffered at my hand."

"My love, I'm not sorry for anything that
happened because otherwise I would be
married to that evil excuse of a man. If

there is anything to forgive, I give it
willingly."

He set her down as if she might break and
scorched his lips on hers in a kiss they
would both remember forever.

One of Eriik's men waited patiently until
Lillian spied him, "Excuse my lady, where
might I put your things?"

Without one bit of embarrassment she said
boldly, "In the lord's chamber, please. My
lord, I would have a word."

They walked hand in hand to his chamber and
when she entered, she sighed. She never
thought she would see this lovely room again
when she was held in Montfort's house of
horrors. She turned and closed the door
quietly, walked over to Eriik, put her hands
on either side of his face and kissed him
with such urgency, it surprised him for a
second, but not one moment longer as he
returned her kiss in kind. She stood on her
toes and wrapped her arms around his neck
and grabbed his long, golden hair, running
her fingers through it, deepening the kiss,
entwining her tongue with his. She could
feel the tingling at the apex of her thighs
and reveled in the beautiful torment. Eriik
picked her up and sat her on the bed as they
started to slowly undress one another. She
was determined to see and feel his naked
body. It was magnificent and it had been
too long since she had laid eyes on the hard
and taught muscles she craved. The long
days in the bedroom at Montfort's she had
dreamed of this day and promised herself if

it ever came to pass she would make it a day
Eriik would never forget and she meant it to
be this day. She was stroking the solid
muscles of his chest and it felt wonderful
but she broke away to caress his groin. He
groaned and started to stop her, he was
afraid since it had been so long, he would
not be able to stop himself from ripping her
clothes off and ramming himself inside of
her and he wanted this to last all
afternoon. She had never murmured the word
before but looked at him with longing, "Let
me touch your cock, my love." That was
indeed his undoing. He had never heard
anything sexual come out of Lillian's mouth
and all he could say was, "my lady." He
held his arms by his side and let her have
her way. She untied his breeches and it was
huge, straining for release. As it sprang
from his trousers, she marveled at its
strength as she wrapped her small hands
around the thickness and length of it. As
she was exploring this wonderful part of
Eriik's body, he was undressing her,
reveling in her flawless body with his
hungry eyes. Her nakedness and fondling was
causing havoc with his senses. "Oh by the
gods you are testing my will, sweet."

She looked at him seductively, and to his
utter amazement she lowered her head and
tasted his cock with her tongue, tentatively
at first then more boldly as she felt his
gasp and then moans of pure pleasure. She
had heard whispers of this act before and
was disgusted, but with Eriik, she was
getting wetter by the second hearing his
sighs of delight. It made her feel powerful
and after all the ecstasy he had given her,

she wanted to make him feel the same way.
She was rolling her tongue around the tip
and down to the shaft and started to feel
quite comfortable with this new way of
loving him when Eriik stopped her, "Sweet, I
must have you, now!"

He rolled her quickly onto her back and
entered her body so slick and wet as gently
as he could possibly manage at this point
and after just a couple of strokes, all of
his great muscles tensed, his face grimaced,
his eyes closed, and he called out Lillian's
name in a roar, then he relaxed just for a
moment, "By the gods woman, you have
bewitched me. I have never, uh, how did you
learn how to…" She put her fingers to his
lips,

"I listen and I learn."

"What has gotten into ya girl?"

"Besides you my lord?" She giggled.

As he laughed with her, she started the
rhythm of the ages, as old as time. She had
held herself in check because she wanted to
hear and feel him completely, but now it was
her turn. He was soft inside of her but she
could definitely feel him and she started to
rock, squeezing her muscles, holding him
inside. She pressed her legs, then relaxed
them. It felt glorious because little by
little, she felt the hardness returning.
Her muscles seized him from inside her body
and he replied with his. They matched one
another stroke for stroke. She arched her
back as she was reaching for a place in the
heavens she knew was there and only he could

take her. He was gathering all his clues from her body and doing exactly what she needed. Slower, faster, whatever she desired, "Eriik, I want to be on top." He spun her on top of him and gently lowered her over him and she celebrated the fullness of him inside her. She began the tightening of her muscles, over and over, again and again. She bent over to give him access to her breasts and his tongue enjoyed the majesty of her erect, pink nipples to excite him even more. All of a sudden, her breath started coming in short gasps, she was close to the precipice, her muscles were grasping his cock in a life or death grip and she would have her way, come what may because she was there. "Oh God, oh my God, yes!" She was trembling and exhausted as she fell on Eriik's chest and placed tiny kisses on his neck and chest, finally navigating up to his lips.

"As I keep trying to tell you my love, I'm only a man," he said laughing."

"I'll have to disagree with you after what I've just experienced."

They both laughed together, Eriik still inside her warmth. She rose up all of a sudden as if she'd forgotten something, "Can you have another?"

"No my dear, I'm quite satisfied. I've exhausted myself and if I tried, you would be walking bowlegged tomorrow."

They both laughed as he gently slid from within her and they held each other into the night. Much later they made gentle, sweet

love one more time before they found sleep
in each other's arms.

Chapter 37

They emerged late the next morning sated from a wonderful night of glorious lovemaking and ready for the day ahead. Unfortunately for Eriik, he had a council he had to attend, "Lillian will you go with me? After the joining ceremony, you will sit beside me and we will make decisions together, after all."

"Of course, I'd love to see how your council works."

After breakfast, they walked to the council dwelling, hand in hand. Eriik seated Lillian as close to him as possible, not being able to sit beside him, not yet anyway. After they were joined, she would be by his side always.

Complaints and problems were brought to the Jarl's attention and he and his advisors solved as many as possible and then Lord Asgaut stepped forward with Helgi at his side.

Eriik had an uneasy feeling.

"Yes Lord Asgaut, what do you say?"

He was practically snarling at Eriik, "I believe Jarl Thorennson, your advisors should hear me, as my complaint is against you."

"State your grievance, then we will make that decision."

"Well, this is a delicate matter. You have lain with a lady, my daughter, Lady Helgi Asgaut, who is with child, your child, a good and true blooded Norsewoman, but I hear you are planning to join with a foreign woman and she will be your wife. This is not of our customs. I understand the ways of the heart, but my daughter should be your one wife and the foreign woman, well…" he shrugged.

"Lord Asgaut, I beg to differ. Lady Helgi is indeed a good and true Norsewoman but you are misinformed, she and I did not lie together and the child she carries is not mine."

The entire room gasped.

"You insult me and mine my lord!"

"I mean no insult, I simply tell the truth."

"No, my lord, you are speaking from your heart."

Eriik stood up with a look of pure rage on his face and Lord Asgaut started to tread closer to the dais.

Lillian silently rose from her seat, causing everyone to stare.

The room quieted and Lillian said simply, "Helgi, Lady Asgaut, if I understand correctly, this is simple. You claim Eriik had relations with you and Eriik, I mean Lord Thorennson claims he did not. I know a sure way to decide who is telling the truth and who is not. Simply describe the shape of Eriik's birthmark to the right of his, uh…"

Helgi erupted furiously, "I will do no such thing. To say anything further than it exists would be absolutely vulgar. No lady would entertain such an unattractive conversation. You claim to be a lady but apparently you are not!"

Lillian simply sat down with the outside of her lips just the slightest bit upturned. No one even noticed, except Eriik.

Lord Asgaut was furious, "Jarl Thorennson, what is the meaning of this outrageous act?"

Eriik seemed amused, "Please pardon my lady, she is trying to untangle this seemingly unsolvable problem."

"How can being rude and offensive solve the problem?"

"Well now let's see, Lady Lillian asked Lady Helgi to describe the birthmark to the right of my uh, well suffice to say on a place on my body one wouldn't ordinarily see. Lady Helgi said she would say nothing further than it exists but would not be ill-mannered and describe it. Is that about it?" He smiled and Lady Lillian smiled back at him.

Lord Asgaut was not pleased, "I don't see anything funny about this. My daughter is a lady who does not stoop to crude conversation, and this is far from solved."

"This has been solved, because you see Lord Asgaut, I have no birthmark."

The room exploded into a roar. Eriik held his hand up to hold down the commotion.

"I hold no grudge against you or your daughter but I suggest you leave this place immediately, find the child's father and inform him of the good news. I will assume you had no knowledge of this fallacy, Lord Asgaut?"

Lord Asgaut appeared stunned, "No, no Lord Thorennson, I swear to you. My daughter will be punished for this, I promise you." Her father took Helgi's arm and dragged her out of the council house none too gently and could be heard yelling at her quite a way down the road.

"If there is no more business, I call this meeting to an end. I'll call for ayes or nays."

All called "Aye."

As Eriik and Lillian made their way back home, Eriik was beaming, "My lady is not only beautiful but very shrewd as well."

"I couldn't lose the love of my life to a pretender."

"And how did you know she was a pretender? How did you know we had not lain together?"

"You told me you had not and I believed you, and that is that."

"What a remarkable woman you are."

Chapter 38

The joining ceremony, or wedding as Lillian
preferred calling it was upon them. It was
Friday, Frigga's sacred day, the goddess of
childbearing. She had obviously already
blessed Lillian and Eriik as two would be
walking down the aisle, instead of only one.
This knowledge made Lillian even happier
than she would have been otherwise.
Carrying Eriik's child was the most wondrous
feeling in the world.

Lillian had asked permission to wear the
wedding gown she had brought from England
from her hope chest and was granted her
wish. They were going to blend the
ceremonies to reflect some of Lillian's
traditions, such as her gown, with the
Norse. The Norse traditions would be upheld
in the fullest, such as the wearing of the
traditional head dress by Lillian. She
insisted it be that way and Eriik was
grateful. She wanted to walk down the aisle
to meet Eriik as she would have done in
England and there was no Norse rule that
prohibited it, so Renouf would stand in for
her father and give her away. He would
provide her with the sword to give Eriik
that would be passed down to their first
born son. Bjorn, standing in as Eriik's
male relative would bring Eriik's sword to
hold high during the ceremony, as well as an
axe, to symbolize Thor's mastery of the
union.

Lillian's gown was white silk and lace with tiny silk buttons that reached down the back of her exquisite gown with lace that reached up to enhance her graceful neck. Alicia was stunned as she helped her dress, "Oh Lady Lillian, you look gorgeous. Lord Thorennson will be swept away by your beauty and charm."

"You're too kind, dear. I expect to be attending your wedding soon what with the rumors I've been hearing. I would be honored to help you when the time comes."

Alicia blushed and whispered, "I can only hope. Oh goodness, it would be my greatest pleasure and honor to have you be a part of my wedding."

"No need to hope, Renouf is smitten with you. Eriik tells me so."

"Really my lady?"

"Of course. Why else would he be working so hard to learn English?"

Alicia blushed as she held up the long train and gasped with delight. She would be following behind Lillian walking down the aisle holding up the yards and yards of silk. Lillian thought perhaps Alicia was almost as excited as she was.

As she heard the beautiful music and the drums, she knew it must be the time she had wished and prayed for all her life, marrying the man she loved.

"Alicia, it is time for me to meet my groom."

The joining ceremony, the wedding, was lovely. The words were beautiful and the presenting of swords was awe-inspiring. Lillian couldn't have been happier and she could tell Eriik was too. Her father had promised she would be allowed to marry for love and in a complicated round-about way he had kept his promise. Perhaps God had helped. However she decided it was most likely Eriik, as he always got his way when he was determined and he had indeed been unwavering in his dogged determination that they be together. She couldn't thank God enough for her wonderful, stubborn Viking.

The feast after the ceremony was fabulous. Everyone in the village turned out and seemed genuinely happy for the couple. By the time they separated themselves from the throngs of well-wishers and managed to get away to their bed chamber, they were more than ready to be alone and find the marriage bed. They were tired but not too weary to make slow, sensual love, savoring every moment as husband and wife, joined for life, and perhaps even after, if the gods deemed it so. Eriik wanted it that way and as Lillian was well aware, Eriik always got his way.

Epilogue

Lillian gave birth to a healthy son with golden hair like the sun and as handsome and strong as his father. No one could have been as proud as Eriik as he showed him off to his kinsmen and villagers alike. One afternoon, while their new son, Lars, was suckling at his mother's breast, Eriik sat down to cuddle both his heart's desires, "What a lucky boy."

Lillian grinned. Her husband was always thinking of ways of the flesh and she was always pleased he was so inclined.

"How I love you my handsome Norseman."

"And how I love you my beautiful wife, my love, my life, my passion, my desire."

THE END